Henry Brereton Marriott Watson

Diogenes of London

And Other Fantasies and Sketches

Henry Brereton Marriott Watson

Diogenes of London
And Other Fantasies and Sketches

ISBN/EAN: 9783337096274

Printed in Europe, USA, Canada, Australia, Japan

Cover: Foto ©Andreas Hilbeck / pixelio.de

More available books at **www.hansebooks.com**

DIOGENES OF LONDON

AND OTHER FANTASIES

AND SKETCHES : BY

H. B. MARRIOTT-WATSON

AUTHOR OF

'THE WEB OF THE SPIDER'

'LADY FAINT HEART,' ETC.

METHUEN AND CO.

18 BURY STREET, W.C.

LONDON

1893

TO

WILLIAM ERNEST HENLEY

THESE PAGES FROM THE

'NATIONAL OBSERVER'

ARE INSCRIBED IN ALL

ADMIRATION AND

AFFECTION

TABLE OF CONTENTS

DIOGENES OF LONDON

'O,' said he, swinging his heels upon the gate and facing the distance meditatively, 'marriage matters nothing. This side of lusty youth love is an affair of arrangement— one down, t'other come on. There is no choice practicable between women. Nonage, I grant you, has delectable idols, but the currents of life sweep us clean of 'em, and when we are come to discrete and uncomplaining years we submit to the maturer laws of our destiny. Marriage,' said he sententiously, 'is of the remotest consequence.'

'I wonder,' said I, 'to find one of so nice a judgment as yourself professing this ungracious creed. You with your past of elegance——'

' 'Tis the past fathers the future,' he broke in : 'I am grown sensible because of this very past. Fop I have been, fop I may endure, but wisdom comes to fops no less than to country squires.'

He gave me a pretty smile as from one upon a superior pedestal ; and somehow he forbade me by

A

it to visit upon him my annoyance that giggling fortune had made him my better.

'This,' said I, 'is a new complexion on your character, and I cannot conceive you in earnest. Your nimble humours dance in my country eyes. You have ever had the repute of a fastidious affection, and this holiday whim consorts not with your town performances. Put your meaning in plain words and be done.'

He shrugged his elegant shoulders, and balanced his cane upon his toe.

'My country droll,' said he, 'it seems my reputation sticks in your throat; it should but prove to you the insignificance of love. These preterite passions would merely argue one of the sex to be as another. Man was the true creation—woman but an afterthought: a serviceable afterthought, I make no doubt,' he said, nodding; 'and her service is greatest in this, that being an appanage she is most economically interchangeable. That,' said he, looking round at me to clinch his argument, 'is the philosophy of the wise, and the earlier you come to it, my rural squire, the better for your comfort.'

''Tis the most wonderful philosophy out of your mouth,' I cried.

He spun a crown in the air.

'Heads or tails!' he called; 'this one or that! Of what consequence? Pooh!' he said.

'This thing is not true,' said I soberly.

He smiled. 'Of what use were it to repeat the proof?' he said. 'You may go take haphazard from the women of the world, and each will make you a mate. It is the question of an hour or two, and, for my own part, to make any business of the choice were unneedfully distressing. This love is an elegant, fine-sounding trifle; but 'tis manufactured by the gross,' he said; ' 'tis manufactured by the gross,' and puffed away his smoke most airily.

'Now,' said I, smiling, 'I have you clearly. If this be your theory, and you will not be at the trouble of choice, it matters nothing whom you wed.'

'Nothing,' said he indifferently. 'For myself, I would engage to marry any of the sex.'

'I give you back your pooh,' said I.

'I am in the mood to convince you,' he replied, with negligence; 'we will put it to the test. I will woo the first comer in petticoats.'

'You will be no such fool,' I answered.

Complacently a smile stole up his face. Yonder!' said he, waving his cane.

Looking down the valley I discerned a speck come crawling up the lane. In a short time it had drawn near enough for reeognition, and presently a halting dame of sixty hobbled by, her nose sniffling the ground. He wavered on his seat.

'At her age she should already be a wife,' said he hesitatingly.

'Or a widow,' said I, who had some knowledge of her. I put my tongue in my cheek. 'Let us consider her a wife,' I said.

He glanced at me distrustfully, and straightened himself with an insensible motion.

'But it shall be the next, I vow,' he said with confidence.

There was no long interval when over the stile before us from the shelving meadows below drew villagewards a youthful figure in a gown of print.

'She has a dainty action on the stile,' I observed with a grin.

He made no answer, but, flinging from the gate, went swaggering across the patch of green into the lane.

'Pray, reconsider,' I called to him. 'This is the rashest venture on important issues.'

'′Tis most immaterial,' he answered lightly. He was a man set in the pink of fashion, and employed his limbs with a delicate extravagance. Stepping into the road, he whipped off his hat and bowed as a true exquisite. The girl stared and lingered, as she brushed the burrs from her skirts. I knew her for the village beauty: one spoiled of whims and vanities, but of a rare spirit and possession.

'Madam,' said he, hat in hand. 'Have you the time of day?'

'The sun is my clock, sir,' she said shortly. 'Gentlefolk have wits as well as we.'

'Nay, only in the singular,' he answered, 'and certainly neither when you are by.'

She flushed, lingering still with the comely gentleman.

'In this vale of tears we have an arduous journey,' he said. 'It has been my fortune to come so far solitary. May I have your company henceforth?'

'I am a poor hand at riddles, sir,' said she, and whirled away bewildered.

Following, he caught her at the turning, and faced her with a solemn countenance.

'You wrong me,' he declared. 'I put no riddle, but a weighty question, to your prettiness. Madam, will you wed me, and prove with me to the world and my obstinate squire that marriage is of the slightest consequence?'

'You are not sober, sir. Sirs, this is a sorry joke,' said she.

'My life, it is most serious,' he vowed. 'Doubtless you would have some information as to my degree. 'Tis a thought worthy of your providence, an exemplar to my sentimentalist behind. These clothes, madam, are of the newest fashion, of a quality becoming to a man of taste and fortune ; and though I am of ordinary clay, I may yet claim to be of fair accomplishments, of an excellent temper, and of a most amusing acquaintance. For my person I say nothing, as 'tis before you at this moment in the correctest of bows,'

wherewith he ducked most magnificently to the
earth.

Her gaze recurred to me wonderingly.

' You are a friend of the squire's ? ' she asked.

' On my soul, madam, I am,' said he, waving at
me. ' But I protest when we are married you
will come to find him a most tedious companion.
Even now he gapes at us.'

Her bosom heaved, and her eyes ran fire.

' I will take your offer, sir,' she said.

He seized her hand. ' Sweetheart,' he cried,
' we will sanctify the bargain,' and at this she
thrust two pretty lips at him.

' 'Tis somewhat in the open,' he declared, ' but
only my decent blockhead witnesses. What!
must you go? Well, then, 'tis all sealed and
settled, and we shall meet anon.'

Slipping from his arm, she tripped down the
lane with face all flushed and sparkling - eyes,
fleeting round the corner precipitantly.

' Go thy ways,' he cried, ' thou dainty bit of
rusticity. Faith, I have touched less delicate lips
and felt a grosser waist.'

Then he swaggered back to me across the green.
' It is a pretty lass,' I said with a chuckle ; ' you
were most fortunate in your selection.'

He was humming a tune, and stopped suddenly:
' I call you to witness,' he said quickly, ' that I
took the chances.'

I puffed at my pipe, astounded to regard this

finished piece of impudent humanity. 'This madness,' I said presently, 'is but of a midsummer
noon. It ends here, doubtless.'

'Gad,' said he, swelling with the humour and
pleased with my serious wonder, 'it ends not here,
nor elsewhere than in the church. Marriage has
been unduly inflated. I have set out to prick
the bubble.' And, lighting his pipe, he fell to
smoking easily.

'Twas on the morrow that I took him most
gravely to task for his folly; but by this he was
captive to his own fancy, and would hear no
remonstrance.

'You put me in mind of my duty,' he said, 'I
had forgot the proper ceremonies of this love.
Faith, I must pay my respects to my sweetheart.
She will look for these usual courtesies.'

When he had returned he reverted to the topic
with the keenest amusement, protesting that she
was an elegant creature.

''Fore Gad,' he said, 'she hath a wit as
ostentatious as her beauty, and a manner to
match.'

A little later I met him walking with her in
the long avenue, and to be sure his judgment had
not been at fault. I had noticed her but little
in my village wanderings, but it was true she was
rarely handsome: misplaced, one would say,
among such rural hinds. He gave me a grand
recognition and passed on, whispering in her ear;

and, turning, I watched him swaggering into the distance.

That night my lord of the neighbouring castle came down from London—a fellow of no pretensions to philosophy, a rude hot-blood of no particular distinction, but seised of many acres and a bountiful rent-roll. Him the mad coxcomb must fill with tales of his troth and rustic lady-love, both laughing over the wine till my lord grew purple between drinking and chuckling, and swore he must inspect the charmer. And it was evident he had carried out his intention ; for they came back next day from a joint excursion, my lord roaring with merriment, and vowing he was ravished by the beauty. For my own part, I could not but think it indifferent usage of the girl, and reflected that my exquisite had in this departed from his wonted taste. The joke promised at this point to endure too clamantly and become the stock subject of our converse ; but somehow it suddenly ceased, and I heard no more of it. Nevertheless, I missed him constantly from my walks, and saw well enough that something was afoot, though he kept a respectable silence about the girl. Once or twice he dropped hints of her, taking pains to say indifferently that she would grace his table mightily, and take the fickle eye of London most uncommonly. He had by this discarded his jesting humour, and I began to think that he had grown uncomfortable (as I had always predicted for him) upon the nearer consideration of his absurd behaviour. But, being determined to show him little mercy for his folly, I suffered him to suppose I looked upon his withdrawal as inevitable, knowing this to be the surest way to keep him to his whimsical purpose. But presently I found his condition to be other than I had imagined.

It dawned on me slowly through a variety of observations. First, he was infrequently in my company, deserting the house often at early morning, and making excuses for his irregular appearances through the day. Then, too, he began to wear the marks familiar in such cases: to smile at space, to murmur to himself, to wander by the garden brook, to take an affectionate interest in flowers, and to shut himself up in his room with an abundance of quills and paper. Each day, whether fair or foul, he declared to be delightful; and whereas before he had often spoken of a return to town, he now swore the country only was inhabitable. But most of all was I astonished and tickled by his bearing to my lord, which soon was noticeable. At the outset merely contemptuous, he came to use his name with so little respect that his own list of vile terms was too meagre for him, and he was fain to borrow from mine. ' A thick-bellied popinjay,' ' a witless moonface,' ' a damned vessel for a damneder title : ' these are poor instances of his abuse. And, indeed, he was

openly uncivil in his presence, and snarled on all
occasions against hereditary honours and fat
pockets. He grew so ill at ease and showed so
much distress that I, who upon learning his state
had been most sardonic in my demeanour to him,
at length forbore in fear of a rupture. And this
was the remarkable condition of things when one
morning near noon he burst suddenly upon my
privacy, his hair unkempt for the first time in my
knowledge, his face betraying a most lively and
ferocious anxiety.

'By God, Squire,' he cried, 'she has gone to
church with your dastard of a lord.'

His fingers twitched, his eyes burned. I took
a pinch of snuff.

'Marriage,' said I, 'my London exquisite, is of
the remotest consequence.'

THE STROKE OF ONE

O Derracott, sunk in his extreme dejection, time had passed like a bird on the wing, and he was already within eyeshot of his house. But now the passage of those footsteps in his wake roused in him a certain vague wonder. He realised that they had seemed to pursue him for some time down the solitary streets; and a little beyond his doorway he halted in the darkness, and turning, awaited curiously the approach of his follower. From his post he saw a figure in the full glory of evening dress pierce the darkness, move sharply into the lamplight, and run briskly up the steps of his own portico. Struck with an amazed alarm, he watched the man insert a pass-key in the lock, and, opening the door, vanish without a sound into the region beyond. The door clicked behind the invader, and Derracott was left staring at the black fanlight. The street-lamp shone upon the desolate area and the vacant wall, but still he stood without a movement on the pavement;

until at length his startled heart stirred slowly,
and the blood flowed down the arteries once more.
With a quick breath of alarm he took a step
towards the portico, stopped suddenly, and gazed
up at the blind windows of the upper stories.
Then with a palsied hand he drew a cigarette
from his pocket, stuck it between his lips unlit,
and, crossing the way, put his elbow on the rails
of the square, and fell into the most tragic
reflections.

This then was to be his welcome from a journey so dismal, and in a mood so desperate. Had
he come upon the morrow, as he had anticipated,
this house had been smiling for him, his wife
bright with a false radiance, and all the consola-
tions of home eloquent of hope and comfort.
Sick at heart from his fruitless mission, he would
have entered upon this rest at the invitation of a
score of specious pleasures. But as it was, the
miscalculation of one day had sufficed to rob him
of this decent refuge; and plunged upon debt
embittered with failure, there was now no longer,
as it seemed, love to forgive him, neither faith nor
courage to inspire and strengthen. And yet of
her at least he had been certain, though his
world else was rumbling in his ears. His gaze
besieged the house as though to tear the walls
asunder and peer into its shameful secrets. His
blood ran now at a charge, and his fingers quivered upon his cigarette. He cast it from him,

and walking precipitately across the road marched up the steps with a thumping heart. As he closed the door the dark silence of the hall dropped like a cloak upon him, and insensibly subdued his actions. His feet made no sound upon the heavy carpet: in his own house he stole with the air and cunning of a thief. Some faculty of restraint had come to his trembling summons, and his breath issued sedately, his pulse fluttered in measured beats, his eyes and ears waited in the silence and the darkness. At the top of the first flight he stopped a moment before his wife's drawing-room, rapped gently with his knuckles, and opened the door slowly.

The room glowed in a soft red light, which illuminated also two stricken faces in the background. The man had risen to his feet and clutched the back of a high chair, his eyes set hard upon the incomer. But it was upon the woman that Derracott's glance fell first. She kept her seat, crouched in the hollow of a large armchair, her face rigid to her lips, her chin twitching to her short breaths, her eyes wild and staring. Mortal terror never sat upon features so spectral; meaningless noises issued from her mouth. Derracott, his cheeks blanched, his muscles strung as upon wires, stepped into the room, and upon this company.

'I have surprised you, my dear,' he said quietly. ' Ah, Harland !' and he nodded to the man.

The woman gave him no answer, but Harland
lifted his hand from the chair, sank into a seat,
and laughed with uneasy harshness.

'Yes,' he returned, 'I'm afraid Mrs. Derracott
is startled. She—— I'd no notion you were
away, and looked in a few minutes ago to see if
you'd give me a game.'

'I saved a day and so I'm here,' explained
Derracott. He stood before the fire and warmed
his hands, his white face stooped to the blaze.
Strange little sounds drummed in his head, but
his fingers spread from his palms without a
shiver. The woman recovered herself with a
short indrawn gasp, rose and moved uncertainly
towards him.

'Why, Teddy,' said she tremulously, 'you have
given me a—a start. But you've got your coat
on'—— and she laid a hand upon his shoulder.

He turned about, but his eye avoided her.

'Ah,' said he, 'I was going to ask you whether
you would allow me to disrobe in your boudoir.'

She laughed hysterically.

'Teddy! of course!' she cried, and fetched up
in a spasm of silence.

He pulled off his overcoat deliberately, and
turned again to the fire without a glance at his
companions. He had to them the look of pre-
occupation, and indeed he was at the moment
abstracted from all definite thought. The sudden
rush of this spectacle, albeit in his fears, had

choked the channels of his mind, and he fell back
tremblingly upon the obvious. He had the vague
desire to stand from this horrible crisis and wait
upon his drowsy will. His nerves strained and
tightened ; his whole body swelled with tension.
The silence struck a fear into the others, and
presently drove the man to speech.

' You 're not very lively, old fellow.' he said with
elaborate cheerfulness. ' Had a bad journey ? '

Derracott turned at last ; his brain was moving.

' No,' he replied after a pause, and with painful
deliberation. ' Pretty fair, but I am somewhat
tired. I had a long day yesterday.'

' Poor Teddy !' said his wife caressingly, and
put out a frightened hand to him.

For the first time since that exchange of
glances upon his entrance Derracott's eyes rested
momentarily upon her face. An obscure and
furtive terror lingered there, and, as his gaze
dwelt steadily upon her, flashed swiftly into open
panic. Her head drooped slightly forward,
poised over against him as a bird before a ser-
pent ; his glance passed on, and touched the man.
Harland was fingering his moustache ; he pulled
out his watch. ' By Jove !' he exclaimed, ' I'd
no notion it was so late. Mrs. Derracott, you
must forgive me. Well, old chap,' and he made
as though to rise, ' you're too tired, I suppose,
for this game, so I'll be off ; I won't keep you
up.'

Derracott's muscles softened ; his body breathed with warm life again.

'Not yet,' he said. 'I'll give you a game before you go. Only my wife had better go to bed. Come, Lucy ; it's beyond your hour.'

The woman, straightening herself in her chair, regarded them both with frantic eyes; terror had sat upon her visage since last her husband had looked upon her. She rose with difficulty and opened her mouth. Some cry hung unuttered on that tongue ; some prayer was contained inarticulate behind those scarlet trembling lips. She moved mechanically to Harland with an outstretched hand, stopped, sighed deeply, and left the room without a word. Harland from the edge of his seat watched his host with doubt ; but the grey face of the latter, and his veiled eyes spoke of nothing but great weariness.

'We will drink first,' he said.

He filled two glasses from the decanter upon the table. Harland's hand shook at his lips, but he drained the glass and laughed.

'Now for this game, my boy,' he said cheerfully.

Derracott, whose fingers were playing with his brimming wine-glass, made no response, and Harland examined him anxiously.

'You're very much down, old chap,' he said, after a space of silence ; then he hesitated and his eyes suddenly lightened. 'It's not money

Derracott looked up so sharply that he winced from the glance.

'Yes,' he answered slowly. 'I'm heavily dipped.'

'My dear chap!' cried Harland as with an eager sympathy; and then feeling shyly for his words; 'look here, Derracott,' said he, 'why not let me give you a leg over? Is it much?'

'I don't mind your knowing,' said Derracott, softly; 'I owe you close on five thousand, and there's some twenty thousand elsewhere.'

'Derracott,' said Harland, leaning towards his companion with insinuation, 'cross out that five, and I'll stand in for the twenty.'

The ashes of the fire collapsed in the silence that ensued; Derracott's face never moved; he turned the shank of the glass between his fingers.

'That's a generous offer,' he said.

'Generous be damned,' returned Harland, gaily. 'It's nothing to me, and we're old pals and——'

'Twenty-five thousand, as the market goes, is, I suppose, a generous price for honour,' broke in Derracott with an air of meditation.

The vestiges of colour ran from Harland's cheeks; their eyes encountered across the table; no words passed, but in that mute question and its vacant answer, as it were, the position of the combatants was acknowledged and defined. With a thin breath, almost of relief, Harland waited for the other whose eyes were still upon him. Derracott squared his elbows on the table.

'Yes,' said he, 'and now for this game.' Beneath the calm surface of his manner Derracott was at the white heat of fury. Every emotion in his nature had gone into the crucible of that raging fire. Did his thought flicker upon that wife he had loved so earnestly, the passion that possessed him leapt in flame from his heart; were his embarrassments flashed instantly before him, his fury mounted in crimson tongues. Pent by his fierce jealousy, his mind converging full upon this sudden horror, he sat with quiet eyes and face of stone, stalking ever nearer to his fluttered quarry.

'You will smoke?' he asked at length. Harland shook his head, and Derracott lit a cigarette and blew the smoke thoughtfully through his nostrils.

'I think,' he resumed presently, 'that I ought to make my own rules in this game.' His voice rang with a note of unconcern, even of pleasantry. Harland threw up his hands.

'I have nothing to say,' said he. Derracott rose softly, took some note-paper from a writing-table, and scribbled for some seconds upon it. Then he took the cigarette from his lips and handed the paper across the table. What Harland read was as follows:—

'*I, Edward Derracott, being in the full posses-*

sion of my senses, have decided to put an end to my life. It has become too much to bear. My debts have involved me too deeply, and I am tired of the struggle. I have no strenyth to go on. May God help my wife! Forgive me, Lucy: I have tried, but there seems no way out but this. Let others take warning by my fate. The turf is accursed. God help me.'

Harland inquired of the writer with his eyes, and the latter jerked his cigarette at the ink.

'Let it have verisimilitude,' he said, 'according to your circumstances.'

Harland's jaw dropped suddenly; he shrugged his shoulders and took up the pen. When he had finished he passed the paper to Derracott, who nodded and rose.

'Put it in your pocket,' said he. 'At this hour the gardens will serve our purpose.'

He drew a brace of pistols from a drawer, and motioning to his companion descended the stairs. The chill October moon shone frostily upon the crisp grass of the square as the two made their way in silence to a central bower of evergreens, the pleasant haunt of children at their hide-and-seek throughout the afternoons.

'I think,' said Derracott, in his suave passionless voice, 'that here is the proper theatre for our little comedy.' He handed a pistol to his adversary. 'Twenty-five thousand!' he murmured. 'There is no need of superfluous witnesses. We two can play our own hands. Twenty-five thousand was a generous offer.'

His hand, with its weapon close-grasped hung at his side.

'If you are resolved to end this thing in this way,' said Harland hoarsely, 'there's no help for it. What are you going to do?'

'According to my idea of the game,' said Derracott softly, 'we should have the option of firing at twelve paces or approaching at the signal. You may have observed it was on the stroke of one when we left. Perhaps you will be good enough to take the church bell as a word of command.'

Harland made no answer, but took his station in the open; Derracott put his back against a leafless ash and waited. The moon struck full upon his face; his eyes moved restlessly; his lips whispered inaudibly. The faint sound of a remote clock rose from a distance and vibrated on the stillness. Harland steadied his arm before him, but Derracott stirred not. A moment intervened of dreadful silence—to Harland a space of hours; and then a heavy bell boomed from the clock tower of the church. A pistol cracked, and a withered branch snapped on the ash by Derracott's head. He himself laughed gently and marched slowly forward to the spot where stood Harland waiting for his death. Smilingly he regarded his victim.

'Twenty-five thousand pounds!' said he. 'It

was a notable bid.   But I think my solution was
the better.   My good sir,' he said, ' the exigen-
cies of this game demand that I should be free of
all coroner's courts ; and my hand trembles.   Suppose I offer you the work yourself ?   You would
be more expeditious, I feel sure.   Let us live up
to our papers.'

He held out the pistol ; Harland, his face
sickly white, made a gesture of impatience, and
took it by the butt.   For a second he looked into
Derracott's eyes.   Each had a confession of
suicide in his pocket, and it needed but an instantaneous turn of the wrist, and this smiling devil
had exchanged fates with him.   Harland wavered
for a breath of time ; and then, clapping the
barrel to his heart, pulled the trigger.

The body sank in a heap at Derracott's feet.
He watched it huddle limply among the damp
and yellow leaves ; noted its open eyes and its
pallid moonlit face.   A stain of blood rested on
the lips.   He bent over the dead man : his pulse
throbbed riotously.

' Twenty-five thousand,' he muttered in a thin
dry whisper, ' a generous offer for my honour.'
He laughed.   ' He might have told me before he
went how much he gave for hers.'

He ceased, stared at the stiffening face with a
gasp, drew himself up gradually, and then with a
short cry of horror flung himself upon the muddy
turf, his mouth gaping at the dead.

THE DEVIL OF THE MARSH

I T was nigh upon dusk when I drew close to the Great Marsh, and already the white vapours were about, riding across the sunken levels like ghosts in a churchyard. Though I had set forth in a mood of wild delight, I had sobered in the lonely ride across the moor and was now uneasily alert. As my horse jerked down the grassy slope that fell away to the jaws of the swamp I could see thin streams of mist rise slowly, hover like wraiths above the long rushes, and then, turning gradually more material, go blowing heavily away across the flat. The appearance of the place at this desolate hour, so remote from human society and so darkly significant of evil presences, struck me with a certain wonder that she should have chosen this spot for our meeting. She was a familiar of the moors, where I had invariably encountered her; but it was like her arrogant caprice to test my devotion by some such dreary assignation. The wide and horrid prospect

22

depressed me beyond reason, but the fact of her neighbourhood drew me on, and my spirits mounted at the thought that at last she was to put me in possession of herself. Tethering my horse upon the verge of the swamp, I soon discovered the path that crossed it, and entering struck out boldly for the heart. The track could have been little used, for the reeds, which stood high above the level of my eyes upon either side, straggled everywhere across in low arches, through which I dodged, and broke my way with some inconvenience and much impatience. A full half-hour I was solitary in that wilderness, and when at last a sound other than my own footsteps broke the silence the dusk had fallen.

I was moving very slowly at the time, with a mind half disposed to turn from the melancholy expedition, which it seemed to me now must surely be a cruel jest she had played upon me. While some such reluctance held me, I was suddenly arrested by a hoarse croaking which broke out upon my left, sounding somewhere from the reeds in the black mire. A little further it came again from close at hand, and when I had passed on a few more steps in wonder and perplexity I heard it for the third time. I stopped and listened, but the marsh was as a grave, and so taking the noise for the signal of some raucous frog, I resumed my way. But in a little the croaking was repeated, and coming quickly to a stand

I pushed the reeds aside and peered into the darkness. I could see nothing, but at the immediate moment of my pause I thought I detected the sound of some body trailing through the rushes. My distaste for the adventure grew with this suspicion, and had it not been for my delirious infatuation I had assuredly turned back and ridden home. The ghastly sound pursued me at intervals along the track, until at last, irritated beyond endurence by the sense of this persistent and invisible company, I broke into a sort of run. This, it seemed, the creature (whatever it was) could not achieve, for I heard no more of it, and continued my way in peace. My path at length ran out from among the reeds upon the smooth flat of which she had spoken, and here my heart quickened, and the gloom of the dreadful place lifted. The flat lay in the very centre of the marsh, and here and there in it a gaunt bush or withered tree rose like a spectre against the white mists. At the further end I fancied some kind of building loomed up; but the fog which had been gathering ever since my entrance upon the passage sailed down upon me at that moment and the prospect went out with suddenness. As I stood waiting for the cloud to pass, a voice cried to me out of its centre, and I saw her next second with bands of mist swirling about her body, come rushing to me from the darkness. She put her long arms about me, and, drawing her close, I looked into her

deep eyes.   Far down in them, it seemed to me,
I could discern a mystic laughter dancing in the
wells of light, and I had that ecstatic sense of
nearness to some spirit of fire which was wont to
possess me at her contact.

'At last,' she said, 'at last, my beloved!'   I
caressed her.

'Why,' said I, tingling at the nerves, 'why
have you put this dolorous journey between us?
And what mad freak is your presence in this
swamp?'   She uttered her silver laugh, and
nestled to me again.

'I am the creature of this place,' she answered.
'This is my home.   I had sworn you should
behold me in my native sin ere you ravished me
away.'

'Come, then,' said I; 'I have seen; let there
be an end of this.   I know you, what you are.
This marsh chokes up my heart.   God forbid you
should spend more of your days here.   Come.'

'You are in haste,' she cried.   'There is yet
much to learn.   Look, my friend,' she said, 'you
who know me, what I am.   This is my prison,
and I have inherited its properties.   Have you
no fear?'

For answer I pulled her to me, and her warm
lips drove out the horrid humours of the night;
but the swift passage of a flickering mockery over
her eyes struck me back as a flash of lightning,
and I grew chill again.

'I have the marsh in my blood,' she whispered; 'the marsh and the fog of it. Think ere you vow to me, for I am the cloud in a starry night.'

A lithe and lovely creature, palpable of warm flesh, she lifted her magic face to mine and besought me plaintively with these words. The dews of the nightfall hung on her lashes, and seemed to plead with me for her forlorn and solitary plight.

'Behold!' I cried, 'witch or devil of the marsh, you shall come with me! I have known you on the moors, a roving apparition of beauty; nothing more I know, nothing more I ask. I care not what this dismal haunt means; nor what these strange and mystic eyes. You have powers and senses above me; your sphere and habits are as mysterious and incomprehensible as your beauty. But that,' I said, 'is mine, and the world that is mine shall be yours also.'

She moved her head nearer to me with an antic gesture, and her gleaming eyes glanced up at me with a sudden flash, the similitude (great heavens!) of a hooded snake. Starting, I fell away, but at that moment she turned her face and set it fast towards the fog that came rolling in thick volumes over the flat. Noiselessly the great cloud crept down upon us, and all dazed and troubled I watched her watching it in silence. It was as if she awaited some omen of horror, and I too trembled in the fear of its coming.

Then suddenly out of the night issued the

hoarse and hideous croaking I had heard upon
my passage.   I reached out my arm to take her
hand, but in an instant the mists broke over us,
and I was groping in the vacancy. Something like
panic took hold of me, and, beating through the
blind obscurity, I rushed over the flat calling
upon her.   In a little the swirl went by, and I
perceived her upon the margin of the swamp, her
arm raised as in imperious command.   I ran to
her, but stopped, amazed and shaken by a fearful
sight.   Low by the dripping reeds crouched a
small squat thing, in the likeness of a monstrous
frog, coughing and choking in its throat.   As I
stared, the creature rose upon its legs and dis-
closed a horrid human resemblance.   Its face was
white and thin, with long black hair; its body
gnarled and twisted as with the ague of a thousand
years.   Shaking, it whined in a breathless voice,
pointing a skeleton finger at the woman by my
side.

'Your eyes were my guide,' it quavered. 'Do
you think that after all these years I have no
knowledge of your eyes?   Lo, is there aught of
evil in you I am not instructed in?   This is the
Hell you designed for me, and now you would
leave me to a greater.'

The wretch paused, and panting leaned upon a
bush, while she stood silent, mocking him with
with her eyes, and soothing my terror with her
soft touch.

' Hear!' he cried, turning to me, ' hear the tale
of this woman that you may know her as she is.
She is the Presence of the marshes. Woman or
Devil I know not, but only that the accursed
. marsh has crept into her soul and she herself is
become its Evil Spirit ; she herself, that lives and
grows young and beautiful by it, has its full power
to blight and chill and slay. I, who was once as you
are, have this knowledge. What bones lie deep
in this black swamp who can say but she? She
has drained of health, she has drained of mind and
of soul; what is between her and her desire that
she should not drain also of life? She has made
me a devil in her Hell, and now she would leave
me to my solitary pain, and go search for another
victim. But she shall not!' he screamed through
his chattering teeth ; ' she shall not ! My Hell is
also hers ! She shall not ! '

Her smiling untroubled eyes left his face and
turned to me ; she put out her arms, swaying
towards me, and so fervid and so great a light
glowed in her face that, as one distraught of
superhuman means, I took her into my embrace.
And then the madness seized me.

' Woman or devil,' I said, ' I will go with you !
Of what account this pitiful past? Blight me
even as that wretch, so be only you are with me.'

She laughed, and, disengaging herself, leaned,
half-clinging to me, towards the coughing creature
by the mire.

'Come,' I cried, catching her by the waist. Come!' She laughed again a silver-ringing laugh. She moved with me slowly across the flat to where the track started for the portals of the marsh. She laughed and clung to me.

But at the edge of the track I was startled by a shrill, hoarse screaming ; and behold, from my very feet, that loathsome creature rose up and wound his long black arms about her, shrieking and crying in his pain. Stooping I pushed him from her skirts, and with one sweep of my arm drew her across the pathway; as her face passed mine her eyes were wide and smiling. Then of a sudden the still mist enveloped us once more; but ere it descended I had a glimpse of that contorted figure trembling on the margin, the white face drawn and full of desolate pain. At the sight an icy shiver ran through me. And then through the yellow gloom the shadow of her darted past me to the further side. I heard the hoarse cough, the dim noise of a struggle, a swishing sound, a thin cry, and then the sucking of the slime over something in the rushes. I leapt forward; and once again the fog thinned, and I beheld her, woman or devil, standing upon the verge, and peering with smiling eyes into the foul and sickly bog. With a sharp cry wrung from my nerveless soul, I turned and fled down the narrow way from that accursed spot; and as I ran the thickening fog closed round me, and I heard far off and lessening still the silver sound of her mocking laughter.

E waited till she had passed between the narrow walls of the maze, and then turned to each other.

'We will start on fair terms,' aid I.

'Assuredly,' he answered gaily; 'but I am damnably lame of one foot. Well, if it may not be thus'—and he tapped his sword with an irritating smile of bravado—'any way will serve.'

'You pay a poor compliment to her decision,' I replied with a sneer. 'You may resolve yourself that she has already made her choice.'

'So I understand,' said he with a grin.

'Your leg'—said I: 'she has the eyes of a hawk.'

'And your wits'—said he: 'she has fathomed them at the outset.'

'If you would be insolent, sir——' I cried.

'Gad!' he interrupted me, 'you've a pretty temper, and a most uncommon desire of her. 'Tis true, I've an elegant passion myself; but faith, would you spit yourself in your folly?' and he half-drew his weapon from the scabbard.

30

'This quarrel will keep,' I replied angrily, ' un-
less you would reduce me to your own halting
gait ere we set forth.'

''Sdeath,' said he, purpling, 'you London
popinjay, I'll have you to know, my visitation is
for my own jests only.'

'I think,' said I coolly, 'that this were better
at the back-end of our adventure. Let us patch
a bargain, my fire-eater.'

'It is well said,' he answered quickly : ' on the
sign we start——'

'And separate,' said I.

' Faith, if you take one road, I'll another ; and
that's flat. I've no fancy for your company.'

'Excellent!' I replied ; ' and he that shall arrive
first at the central arbour——'

'Shall ravish a kiss of her, by my body,' quoth
he.

'And,' I added, ' be taken for her lover.'

A voice broke softly on our talk, and wheeling
we saw a kerchief tossing in the air.

'That is our signal,' said I.

But he was already gone, and in a twinkling I
was after him. I caught him at the first turning
in the maze, whence two tracks started abruptly
in opposite directions. Without a pause he
whisked into the left. 'Her skirts,' thought I,
'flashed round this corner as she went,' and
chuckling made off by the right. The privet
hedges rose high, so that he disappeared from my

view immediately; but, keeping the central ash
in my eye, I ran on. The maze twisted marvel-
lously, ran in astounding little circuits, and dodged
hither and thither in an utterly preposterous
fashion. I had no judgment by which to go,
save my own vague discretion; and though at
first I took my resolutions on the run, and with
the easy confidence of novelty, soon—finding myself no nearer to the arbour, but somewhat hot
and breathless with my speed—I began to choose
more leisurely, and with an air of observation.
Where each way branched I paused and meditated;
reckoned up the chances; cast a few calculations
in my mind; and drew what inference seemed
likeliest. In the distance I could hear my rival
tramping along, but it was not until I had been
some ten minutes at my task that he came into
my neighbourhood. He was separated from me
by several fences, but, to my chagrin, was upon
the inner side and evidently nearer to our common
goal. I had regained some breath, and, happen-
ing at the moment upon what struck me as an
admirable clew, I was spurred, at once by his
seeming good fortune and my new hopes, into a
quicker pace. Presently, rounding an arm of the
hedge, I plumped into a stranger whose presence
in the place I had not looked for. He was an
old man, with large infantine eyes and a beard of
venerable white, and he was ambling along with
a paltry, nervous gait, resembling that of a

perturbed child. So much embarrassed was I at the delay of this accident that I had forgot my manners, and with an expression of impatience was making off, when he clutched me by the coat.

'I pray you,' said he in a piping voice, 'I pray you, kindly direct me to the issues of this lamentable prison.'

'At your age,' said I, 'you should know better than to be at this ridiculous game;' and, thrusting him aside, I pushed on at a hot speed.

But I had no better luck from my latest inspiration, and was becoming annoyed by the persistent rebuffs of fortune. Indeed, I seemed ever to be choosing the particular path which ended in a great blank wall of privet; and the greater part of my time was expended in withdrawing from the absurd predicaments I had created for myself. Of my rival I had now no news, but was assured that his incompetence was equal to mine by the mere fact of his silence; for though I had no doubts that he would be swearing loudly enough were he within hearing, it was as certain that he would inform me of his success by some braggart noise, did he penetrate into the interior before me. While losing heart after this fashion, it was my luck to fall across the belated ancient once more. He was biting his finger-nails reflectively, and wore a very distressful appearance. On hearing my approach he whipped round and brightened visibly.

c

'Sir,' said he, with a manner of pleading diffidence that sat ill on his years, 'I perceive you to be well acquainted with this delightful puzzle. In my young days I had the same knowledge and took the same delight. But I have grown staider and (God help me!) somewhat stiff of joint. My wit misguides me; and having the misfortune to have wandered in here after a meritorious butterfly, I should be deeply honoured by your condescension in putting me upon my way to the exit.'

He spoke very formally, and with an urbanity that would have been pitiful had I been less moved by my own troubles. It was plain he was exceedingly anxious to be gone.

'Let us strike a bargain,' said I. 'You have come from within; I am from without. You shall direct me to the arbour, and I in return will send you to the gates of this infernal place.'

'With pleasure,' said he eagerly. 'If you will bear henceforth to the right you will come shortly to the centre.'

I had not the remotest desire to mislead him, but he might certainly as well pursue my random directions as his own; and I could do no less than make him some return for his information: so I answered promptly enough.

'And you,' said I, 'if you will keep to the left, will come out upon the lawn.'

I was itching to be off on the new experiment, and, ere he could thank me, was gone. I had

procceded but a little further, when by some sorry
trick of Fate's I stumbled on my fellow drawn up
in an opening of the privet, and looking hot and
discomfited. I had no mind that he should stick
at my heels; and so, lest he should observe the
triumph in my eyes, I stopped, and dissembled
my features into a proper grimace of despair.

'You have been no nearer than this?' I
asked. He mopped himself and ejaculated an
oath.

'The thing has no end, neither beginning,'
he said.

'We are in the same case,' I answered; 'but,'
said I cheerfully, 'we must push on, we must
push on. Hope is our portion, my friend, in all
desperate emprises.'

'Pish!' said he. 'I've no stomach for this
eternal hedge of privet. Give me a plain field,
and I see my way. These walls are fit only for
your puling citizen.'

'True,' said I. 'They have an air of monotony; but one may suffer much in so amiable a
cause. You withdraw, then?' I asked him.

'Faith, not I,' he returned; 'not without your
company;' and eyed me obdurately. 'But,' says
he, 'one way is as good as another. Right or
left?' and he spun a guinea in the air.

'If you will adventure your chances upon such
a hazard——' I said, and shrugged my shoulders.
'For myself, I prefer the guidance of my own

shrewd wit and observation. I wish you a pleasant journey.'

I left him spinning his coins with a red and sweating brow, and made off with all speed.

In a very little I perceived I was approaching to the centre, and my heart beat high with exultation; which grew well-nigh ecstatic when I came into a circle that left me divided by but a single hedge from the arbour and my divinity. And then fell the suddenest blow to my gay expectations. For the path ran half-way round the central opening and there ended in a wall. Mortified beyond the faculty of speech, I stared at this miserable impediment to my prospects, incensed with the old dotard who had so cheated me. At this moment a voice called me softly by name, and through the interstices of the privet I could just espy the sweet face of my lady—the object of all this arduous adventure. I assumed my best grace and bowed to the privet.

'Madam,' I said, 'there is still a barrier be-tween us. But I vow I am rewarded for this tedium of solitary wandering by the mere glimpse of your face which I catch between leaf and leaf of these bushes.'

'You are vastly complimentary,' said she, and laughed.

'My dear,' I replied, 'at least I am more privileged than my rival, who is now, one must suppose, tossing away his chances somewhere on the outskirts of this merry maze.'

'"Tis no fault of mine,' said she demurely.

'He is lame of a leg,' I rejoined.

'Oh !' said she.

It was not my desire to enlist her heart on his behalf, but only to discover to her the cruel embarrassments of our common condition. Therefore I said no more of him, but turned to myself. 'And I,' I continued, 'am out of breath and spent with much running. I have put on the speed of a racer, and have covered many leagues since we last met.'

'I am very sorry,' says she softly.

From her voice I imagined she showed some signs of relenting, and so fetched up at my subject. 'Between this walk and your own sweet person,' 'I said, 'are many leagues more. How many and how arduous the Devil alone knows that built this horrid circus.'

I thought she sighed.

'Thus,' said I, ''twixt you and me are many weary hours of effort, and I am in a plaguey condition of famine. Exhaustion has done its worst upon me. Dearest, I shall have no hope of reaching you.'

I could espy a flush of colour in her cheek; she sighed and plucked at the privet.

'I beseech you, therefore,' I went on, 'to reconsider your edict. I have done much, I have fared far, I have fought well. Sweetheart, there is now but one wall between us. By all the love—— '

'If you desire,' she broke in suddenly, 'the secret of the maze, on my soul you shall not have it.'

She took me aback with her abrupt resolution, ensuing upon a mood of apparent tenderness. I rose to a fury.

'Then,' said I passionately, 'on my soul I will hack through this accursed privet.'

I drew my sword out of its sheath; and she, her eyes blazing with indignation, put her face to the crevices and fixed me with an imperious look.

'Shame on you!' she said. 'You would win by fraud and force what you cannot by an industrious intelligence. Be patient ere you be bold.'

What I should have answered I know not; at the moment I was like to have disdained her rebuke, and set upon the hedge. But just then I heard a piping voice, and the troubled face of the old dotard peeped through the chinks at me from beside her.

'In God's name,' I cried, 'how got you there?'

''Twas your direction,' he mumbled reproachfully. 'By keeping to my left I am come back at your instance to a place from which I had

already thanked God for deliverance. Sir, you
have not played me fair.'

'Well,' said I, grinning, 'and you have tricked
me also, you misguiding prophet!'

The situation tickled me even through my
anger. I put up my sword and laughed.

'Farewell,' I said, 'old totterer! Gad, I envy
you your place and proximity.'

With that I turned and fled, for I had now
the key of the riddle in my hands. To retrace
my steps to the spot on which I had encountered
the old man, and thence to follow my own casual
directions, was now my clear course, and one that
promised an immediate reward. It was with a
light heart I pursued my way, reverting upon my
old tracks. But, alas! it was to little purpose.
The place had vanished, and I was no nearer
finding it after an intolerable deal of travelling.

Thus occupied, and thus filled with a rare
spleen, I happened upon my limping companion
in this hopeless quest. We stopped as by a
common thought on the verge of two paths.

'You are heated, it seems,' said he, panting.

'And you,' I retorted, 'have the sweat of a
labourer.'

'Granted,' said he, and paused. 'This is a
devil of a business,' he added, with a grimace.

I was very tired and dusty, and inordinately
savage; I could have whipped out my sword and
attacked him.

'I have tossed for hours,' said he, 'and it has brought me no nearer — not within scent of her.'

'I have seen her through the hedge,' said I; and have had a mighty pleasant talk with her.'

He seemed to consider, and then laid his hand on his sword.

'There was something we were to discuss,' says he. 'This is a convenient place.'

'To be sure,' I answered. 'An admirable thought!'

We bared our weapons.

'Stay,' said he suddenly, scrutinising the ground. 'Do you recognise the spot?' he asked. He walked off to the furthermost limit of the curve, and presently came limping back.

'We set out both with an exemplary passion for this lovely creature,' says he, looking at me very comically.

'Well?' said I, seeing he was to proceed.

'A girl,' he went on, 'who has enclosed herself within the Devil knows how many walls is in some sort sacrosanct. Her virginity demands respect,' says he.

'Well?' said I.

'And one that exacts as much sweat and worry of a lover as may be got out of the most desperate battle is in some sort a vixen,' says he.

'True,' said I.

'Then,' says he, 'what say you? There is an elegant and most refreshing brew at mine host's in the village; and faith, the exit, as you will perceive, lies below us.' He jerked his thumb down the circle.

'Agreed,' said I suddenly; and, slamming down our swords into their scabbards, we linked our arms and marched abreast out of the maze upon the greensward.

THE HOUSE OF DISHONOUR

THE wind was a roaring tenant of the desolate chambers, and scurried through the house, filling the long bleak corridors with the sound of its furious passage. Out and aloft it screamed most melancholy in the pines, and flew round the corners and gables in claps of passion. The white night seemed in the possession of a thousand evil powers that mocked my solitary watch by her bedside. Anon her soul would flicker to her eyes; the lips would tremble; the lids would rise, and the slow unmeaning gaze rest for an instant upon me. And then again the lashes would fall, and life, impotent and weary, would droop and vanish from the beautiful clay. At that hour I felt no terror for my grievous sin; as we had loved so also had we lived—and the record of those few poor months was sacred to me. No distant thought of my wife came to me oversea; I had put her from my mind long since with the great sin that was my happiness. In that hour but one hope held me,

but one fear. Without, the long drive ran upwards through the ragged woods towards the hills,
and by that avenue must come the aid I looked
for against this Death that shrieked about the
house and wandered whining through the empty
rooms. My glances strayed between that silent
couch and the bare, shining road, my heart beating with fear as though it were I, not she, that
drew nearer to the end. And, in truth, not she
but I was wrestling with this spectre. In my
thoughts I heard him crying in the night; I
watched him on his rounds; between him and the
the dying, I the living stood defiant—of my love
I braved him there alone that night within the
darkness. And, swollen to a monstrous horror,
Fear kept me company, and all past delight, all
future evil, laughed me to derision in its presence.
Apart sat the one servant left me who had not
fled that pest, a faithful guardian at the door,
immediate to the slightest call, should any call
sound here save that of Death above the noises
of the night.

I could not catch her breathing; she opened
her eyes in a smile, and the white teeth shone
spectral in the twilight of the room. I bent to
her shuddering—there was some whisper on those
wavering lips, but the wind was gibbering like a
devil at the windows.

'To steal the last whisper,' I cried, ' that were
worthy of God ! ' and hid my face upon the couch.

It was at this instant there fell a sudden hush, and through the distant doorway he entered swiftly with the sharp clank of spurred feet. Turning, I beheld him white and furious against the light.

'You have a cunning turn for escape,' said he, 'but it will not serve you long. Put a hound to the scent, and in the end he will lick his chops in blood.'

'Hush !——' I cried; but swifter than my swift voice he flung between me and my words.

'Coward!' he said, his jaw fixing upon the cry, and, raising a heavy hand, came in a stride upon me. I took him by the wrist, and besought him with my eyes.

'Hush——,' said I, and the voice choked in my throat so that I could but point a shivering finger to the couch and my white lily drawing unto death.

'What is this?' said he, and stared upon me.

'The Plague,' I muttered; but my words were low, and I seemed to speak to myself.

His white face was so close to mine that I could mark each line time had turned upon his cheeks, and I thought that his black eyes grew blacker, and a slow smile wrinkled about the moving lips. He said no word, but, walking to the bed, peered down upon his sister where she lay. I seemed to see her fading in and out of consciousness, as it were, with her heaving bosom, and her eyes

I thought met his with that plaintive look of suffering that had tortured me through the long day. If this were so I know not surely, for at that moment the gravel rang with a clatter of hoofs, and, at the sound, I sprang towards the door. Then there broke in my old and faithful servant, and the wind flapped down upon us from the sky. I heard his voice calling through the noise, his thin hands gesticulating in the air; and at his words I stood struck dumb and cold.

'No help!' he cried, 'no help!' Nothing will avail now. The plague has taken the very servant on his errand,' he moaned; 'the plague! the plague!'

And, looking through the long windows, I could espy in the white night a great horse steaming from the nostrils, and a limp figure sprawling from the stirrup, stark and motionless.

I think I was now quit of my senses, for I turned and took the brother by the coat. 'Man,' I said, 'ride as from Hell. Ride for this physician beyond the hills, and God will be with you upon this errand of pity. Ride!' I cried. He shook me off and laughed.

'Sir,' said he, 'you have mistaken. I am no serf or bondman of yours, but the mere brother of this pitiful creature who is like to redeem somewhat of our honour within this night.'

At these monstrous words I fell back, staring at his white and smiling face.

'Why,' said he lightly, 'you will perceive the

situation.   These six months I have been minded
to dissolve this pretty compact; and but that
you hid yourself so deftly these hands had surely
done it.   But now the task is taken from them ;
she will herself dissolve it forthwith I doubt not.
It is a sure way out of a mighty unpleasant case.'

He stood twiddling his thumbs and smiling
at me.

'This is an ill time for a jest,' I cried, finding
voice at last.   'Ride, ride ! for the devil is behind
you.'

'I regret,' said he, 'to find you at a loss for
reason.   You have no eye for logic at this
moment, but it is obvious that your vision will
be clearer by-and-by.   You have a pleasant
home,' said he, glancing through the window,
'but a trifle noisy on a windy night, and lonely
in the time of plagues.'

'God who made you,' said I hoarsely, 'judge
you for this !'

'I am the brother of this thing,' said he, jerk-
ing his finger at the couch, 'that soon shall be a
corpse.   With that she will have passed beyond
the dishonour of our honourable house.   And yet,'
he continued, as though at a sudden thought,
'though she be no wife of yours, I have hopes
you will conduct her obsequies in the decorous
fashion of your race.   It is said you toll the
death-bell in these hours of dissolution.   Though
the plague have rid you of your domestics, I

perceive a serviceable veteran here whom, doubtless, you will instruct in this proper ceremony.'

He paused as though for an answer, but I,
speechless with horror and a growing madness,
crouched back against the wall.

'You are uncivil in your silence,' he resumed.
'No doubt it were distasteful in your eyes to
treat your mistress as your wife. And yet you
will pardon me if, out of respect for what is still
the dying body of my kinswoman, I take upon
myself to order this ceremony upon your behalf.'

He had scarce ceased ere I had flung upon him;
but at that very second the life surged in my love
once more, and with an inarticulate cry she raised
her head. I threw him away and fell upon my
knees beside her. Her breath went soft upon my
cheek; her bosom palpitated and was still.
Springing from the room, I rushed out of the
house and leapt upon the panting horse before
the door. Loosened by my leap, the plague-
stricken, dusty body slipped from the stirrup and
rolled full into the moonlight upon the gravel.
I dashed my hands at the reins, spurred at the
reeking beast, and faced the night bareheaded,
clattering for the cliffs. The horse, overworn
with the hard riding of her dead master and
smitten, maybe, with something of the panic of
that fearful countryside, shivered and trembled
on her way. The fire was gone from her palsied

limbs; her life was spent; her fore-legs splayed and staggered on the hard chalk ; and stumbling from point to point we rolled together through the night.   The winds now flew from all quarters upon us, and stung my sight so keenly that the lids fell with the quick pain.   Out of the sea below they seemed to rise up and take the beast below her belly, lifting her from her traitor feet. From the front they sprang at her, chill and gusty, choking the hot breath back into her gaping throat.   While ever from the black hills they dashed upon us both as though to swirl us in their company over the sheer cliffs, where the white sea ran shouting upon the walls below.

In this helpless fashion I had gone but a mile or so, and was come to where the mountain closes on the sea and leaves but a ribbon of pathway, when I was aware of a rider thundering in my rear.   So great was his speed that I had but turned uneasily in my saddle when he swept by me ; his pallid face gleamed for an instant in a set and cruel stare, and then he was past the corner in the distant gloom.

'Ride! ride!' I called ; and my weak steed, struggling with the wind, followed behind him into the narrow pass.   The great circle of the moon hung upon the sheer heights, and the silver streak of footway ran white along the cliff-verge. I had imagined him a penitent, assured that some grievous exhibition of his sister's plight had at

last made a call upon his humanity; and that he
was thus tardily upon mine own errand.   But as
I entered upon the passage I perceived him standing there in the moonlight, his face turned full
upon me, his horse at hand oblique across the
pathway.   As I rode up he raised an arm and
checked me.

'Upon second thoughts,' he said, 'I cannot
perceive that the performance of her manifest
duty acquits me of mine own.   You will dismount.'

I gazed at him in stupefaction across the
vapour from my horse's nostrils.

'Come, you are dull, you are dull,' he went on
impatiently.   'You must know the consideration
proper to her blood.   Be done with your wonder
and dismount.   I have given the matter careful
thought, and believe me it is the one thing
possible.'

It was then for the first time I took his meaning, and the full significance of his hideous purpose flashed upon me.   Passion choked my voice.

'Out of my way!' I whispered hoarsely.

'Descend,' he said; 'or shall I break this
creature under you.   You make an uncommon
fuss.'   He took a pistol from his belt.   'Into the
care of this,' said he, 'I have put my honour.
Come.'

I ground my teeth and clenched my hand
above my head.

'Out of my way, devil!' I cried, pushing the horse's nose upon him.

He put it aside.

'Nay,' said he easily, 'you may perhaps ride on hereafter if you have the occasion left you. By my soul, we must settle on this spot, if I should pull you from the saddle. Your mistress shall find a fitting burial, I promise you, in the tail of the morrow. Dismount, my craven!'

The madness rushed upon me in a flood, and I bent low upon my horse's neck.

'Out of my way!' I repeated.

He laughed. I struck my heels deep in the flanks, and with a start the beast leapt forward upon the white face in the path. His horse behind him swerved and pulled, backing upon the cliff. The winds dropped from the heights in a gust. Spurring, I drove at him. I saw the fore-feet of my horse poised in the air a moment, and then with a plunge she flung herself free upon the empty path; while with a sharp neigh of terror that other creature rolled in a tangle with the white, set face, slipped o'er the verge, and fell from peak to peak down the great precipice below.

And at that instant the shrill wind came crying round the pillars of the hills, and I could hear far off and desolately still the sound of a dull bell booming through the night.

HE took me by a button of my coat, and pulled me round till his serious eyes were upon the level of my own. It was pretty clear he was disposed to convert me from my waggery; and though I had little enough stomach to play the confessor, there was something in his gravity that reduced me to attention.

'You are a man of much knowledge,' he said very soberly. 'I am but a tyro. Yet I would consider passion to be a common faculty of the race, identical at all times and in all conditions, nothing bettered by your superior wisdom, nothing cheapened by my scanty years. It is not upon the passion I would consult you; I would have your advice upon its conduct, which is a matter of experience.'

'Will you hear nothing against your scheme?' I asked.

'I have no scheme,' said he; 'I have only a desire. It is you that shall devise me a scheme.

As to the desire let us be silent; you and your knowledge have no concern with it.'

He was so single-minded in this silly fancy of his, and fronted me with so courteous a dignity, that I could not refrain a smile; he might have been issuing the ultimatum of a nation, and not the trumpery protest of love at five-and-twenty.

'Why,' said I, 'you put a heavy responsibility upon me. You ask me to give the whip to a beggar's horse. The devil is an intolerable fortune for so promising a lad.'

The determination slackened on his face, and his eyes, relenting, took on a cast of fear lest I should take part against him.

'But you have seen her,' he said quickly. 'You admit her beauty. I shall meet no devil, I vow. She has grace and charm and loveliness and fascination. What further excellence would you have in her?'

I was in no mood to discuss his lady, but was thus driven to make good my case by an objection.

'These things are all one,' I said. 'Listen to the voice of a lover! We have said she comes of an inferior class. She is pretty; but she inspects the world from a very different corner. I doubt if your views overlap in any particular.'

'It is nothing against her,' he cried; 'mine shall go nearer hers'—(I shrugged my shoulders) —'or hers shall touch mine. Give me a start,' he said, 'and tell me of your abundant experience how she may be won.'

'She will have none of you?' I asked.

'She is so indifferent that she will barely recognise my presence,' said he.

I laughed. 'Put on your spurs; put on your spurs,' I said. 'You shall gallop if you will, though you should blaspheme for it later.'

'You have always been my friend,' he said, and snapped eagerly: 'how shall I start? Fit me with the boots, and you shall hear of me no more.'

'What sort of girl is this?' I asked with a chuckle.

It was a ridiculous question, I own, and started him upon a glib panegyric, which I interrupted with a gesture.

'And there is more to follow,' he said, eyeing me with a certain shame and a little reproach.

'God forbid!' I answered. 'We have already here the raw matter for a dozen angels. We do not desire to people Paradise, but to fashion one ninny of a woman for sober contemplation. With all this appreciation has she never a look for you?'

'Never a thought,' he returned promptly, 'and but idle looks.'

'Your wealth?' I asked.

'She is innocence itself,' he said, 'and my money weighs with her nothing. Besides, she

has a passion for the romantic, and would con-
temn it.'

'A convenient passion,' I said, musing : 'the
cleanest weapon in the world against a maid. If
you should rescue her ?'

He threw up his hands. 'Where is the possibility ?' he demanded. 'Fires or bulls, rivers
or thieves, runaway horses or libertines—I have
prayed for them daily; but life is flat and un-
adventurous; and London is a city of damnable
good order.'

'Disorder may be contrived,' I suggested.

'The trick is stale. I have purchased a man
in his cups for the office,' he declared bitterly;
'I gave him a crown and the weight of my fist.
It was a vain adventure.'

'It did not move her ?' I asked.

'She turned to me very prettily with her
thanks,' he said. 'O yes, I have her gratitude.
But her gratitude !' He elevated his brows.
'She thinks I have an admirable muscle ; but so
have a dozen in her acquaintance.'

'You would not balk at a lie ?' I asked.

'I would take any fence on the road to her,'
he replied with ardour. 'If you have hope——'
He gazed at me inquiringly.

'Why not,' said I, 'design a situation of the
sentimental ? Would she yield to low lights or
the warm juxtaposition of a carriage. These are
occasions potent against a woman's independence.

Her affections are not obdurate, nor is her will ; they need but the proper circumstance to melt. Women have no power of withdrawal. Take 'em to the brink, and they go over with giddy heads. The brain swims, and they topple to their fate. Man flows in a current, woman in eddies. Her heart is a jewel within the reach of any cutpurse apt enough with his sentences. My dear sir,' I said, ' this is the sexual distinction. For a man's head is approached through his heart ; but a woman's heart is exposed by the swimming of her brain. If you will make a study of her tastes you shall contrive a surrender within the month.'

' Give me the secret,' he said earnestly.

' You forget,' said I, ' I have no knowledge of her quality.'

' And I,' he sighed, ' am a dunce at such riddles. You shall make her acquaintance,' he said quickly.

' Rather,' said I, smiling, ' you shall explain her to me. She is a woman and therefore can admire. In what pose can you swagger at your best ? '

' I have cut all my figures,' he said moodily.

' You are a man of letters,' I said : ' will this serve ? '

He shook his head. ' I propped myself upon the lie and it broke. She has no regard for letters.'

'You paint?' I queried.

'The pretence were useless,' he returned dolefully. 'Her art is upon the hoardings.'

'It would seem, my young lover,' I said, 'that your affection is gross enough to sneer. But suppose yourself an orator upon a tub, or a budding politician.'

'The premier and my lord the duke—she has heard of them,' he replied bitterly.

'Come now, you fight—bluejacket or red,' said I. 'You can entertain her with fine tales of blood.'

He swore a little. 'She inquired upon the point on our earliest acquaintance, and I had the folly to be honest.'

''Twas unfortunate,' I answered; 'but there are finer coats than upon a soldier. Come, the truth. You are the heir of a great family, awaiting your title.'

''Twill serve me as little as my money,' said he. 'She is an excellent girl,' he cried, with an access of rapture. 'Egad, neither wealth nor position touches her.'

'We must take commoner weapons against her,' I said. 'It is idle to menace a savage with fire-arms. Letters and art, politics and culture—she meets them with a stare. Do you not see in what terms you are condemning the little jade?'

'I love her,' he vowed sullenly.

'Well, well,' said I; 'and so shall she love

you. Take heart, young wiseacre, and give ear.
For this, I make no doubt, is a maiden with the
faculty of worship; and that she will not take
virtue to her heart is plain enough. None of her
sex has fallen in love with a virtue: which, moreover, will always prove too modest and reticent
for advertisement. Nay, you must caper at
something to catch her eye and humour; and if
art and its fellows be too high for her, you must
descend upon a lower stage. And there's the
word,' said I : ' the stage ! You must rant and
roar it in the gay plumage of a melting melo-
drama. Ravish away her ear and her eye, and
you 'll have the heart bowling after to catch ' em
up.'

'The playhouse,' said he sadly, 'is denied her
by her parents, and I should stalk there till the
crack of doom.'

' The stage,' I answered, ' is not the sole cyno-
sure of the day. The senses of these women go
down in homage to the spectacle in the streets.
Clap your hands, yell, pull wry faces, gibber and
jest, make the street ring with you; strike
through eye or ear, through some sense, through
a main avenue, to fame ; be foremost in a public
gaze; tickle with primary colours ; bedazzle with
flaming hues ; rehearse heroic gestures and pose
illustrious in a people's face—fill the moment or
the hour, somehow, somewhere, sometime ; and
your goddess will kneel to you in tears. Go

forth and grin about the city like a dog. 'That,' said I, ' is how she shall be conquered.'

He had heard me out with manifest impatience, and now addressed me with some heat.

'Your experience of the sex, sir,' said he, ' would seem to have been sufficiently damnable. I condole with you,' and, turning upon his heel, made off.

I saw nothing more of him for weeks, and it was not until the recent exhibition in the city that I witnessed the end of this farce. Some merry cousins from the country were bent upon the Show, and I was fain, out of good-nature, to accompany them. As the procession passed I espied with some surprise the girl of our discourse leaning from an opposite window, her pretty face flushed and smiling, her eyes betraying the liveliest enthusiasm. I could not but reflect upon the justice of my young friend's commendation, and, following her gaze, my own lighted upon the man himself in a most unexpected quarter. He was seated upon the foremost car in the procession, the topmost figure in a portentous group, swathed in rainbow colours and great whirling garments ; and he was fitted with a crown. He was meant, I understand, for some representation of Victory, and his face beamed with the pride of conquest.

He had the grace to offer me his thanks upon his wedding-day.

THE THING IN THE COPSE

MELANCHOLY silence held the nether wastes as I came down upon the back of the village. I had no thought of horror or remorse; no revulsion turned me from the sober contemplation of that still, stiff figure in the copse, its eyes open upon the dusk unmeaningly. It was true the thing bobbed in and out of my mind persistently, as though that fell moment of fury had stamped an indelible picture on my brain; but its motions had come to be well-nigh mechanical, and it was only at intervals I was aware that it was dancing there. Flitting as a speck in the eyesight, it was no distress to me; I had no care lest it should come a permanent visual sensation. Of the dread itself I recked nothing; there was no relic of hatred in me for the strewn and helpless body, nor any fear of its particular vengeance. I had put from her for ever (it seemed to me) the material object of her shame and madness; and though my soul now should keep the earth until the crack of doom,

it should have the solace of her desolate company. In vain, after all, had she turned from me; the empty world gaped for her now as it had done for me since that terrible hour two nights gone. The horrid glee of this reflection ran through my veins, but no malignity for the dead or for the living had part in my peculiar joy. Indeed, now he had withdrawn from the possibility of her touch, and there was no longer the mocking picture of her delicate caress, I seemed to myself clean rid of animosity against him; and that last thought of admiration which had flashed so strangely upon me at the supreme moment of his fall recurred to my newly dispassionate mind. I would not deny him a fine courage and a rude air of distinction; he had made no craven struggle in his end, but dropped softly in the long ferns without a word, gone to his shameful account unwincingly.

The steep thin track, banked and over-arched with the gloom of deep thickets, widened upon a sudden in a place of heaving yews. The winds brushing round a corner in the downs swept past me upon the deep valley, raising a dismal singing in the pines. Against the low lights of heaven the still, black body with its open eyes tossed and swayed, and low noises were growing in the long corn, when from the darkness of the lower reaches she fluttered into my sight. She came as a white shadow of skirts out of the heart of the rustling

thicket, but I knew her on the instant in that
blackness, as I have ever known her by her mere
proximity.   I was acquainted with her errand,
too; for he had thrust a gibe at my frenzy; and
where he had waited for the tryst, there had he
perished.   Standing in the centre of the way, I
watched her draw near; she came with a start
and a slight cry; shrank into the shadows; moved
as to pass me swiftly; then, pausing, she raised
one arm across her face and bowed her head upon
her moving bosom.   I could not discern her
features ; but the lithe grace of her familiar body
leapt into possession of my soul.   The black
Thing dangled in my eyes upon the trees—I took
a step to her and saw her face, the face that had
touched mine so often, aghast with fear and
shame.   Could sorrow turn that laughing face to
this pallid spectre of loveliness ?   I had not seen
her since that hour when I had all but thrown
her from the Hall into the windy night.

' You!' said I tensely.   'You!'

She put out her hands, as it were in a gesture
of despair, still bowed and mute.   I looked upon
her in the falling dusk as mute as she, and the
memory·of her invisible beauty made a chasm in
my thoughts.

' It is no use to speak of pardon,' she whispered
at last, the dear, tremulous whisper that had been
wont to murmur at my ears; 'I have come too
low for pardon.   It is only pity that I ask.'

'Pity!' I echoed, blinking at the black Thing that tossed about her head.

'There were some excuses for me had I the shamelessness to name them. I was mistaken in myself. My mother—I had seen little of you, save that you were great and noble. A girl's fancy—a girl's blunder—and my mother——'

'Twelve months married,' I murmured; 'but twelve months.'

'I fought for you against myself and him,' she said. 'God knows I fought—but in a little——'

'Twelve months,' I murmured; 'but twelve months.'

'I was too weak for my own passions. God knows, who made us, why such passions are poured into weak vessels.'

'Some for dishonour,' I said: 'some for dishonour.'

'You were too high for me. I never knew you. You had stern moods. I could not reach them. Love turned to fear of you. I was afraid, and betrayed you in my fear. Yours was not the heart of a lover.'

'Your breath was the spirit of my body,' I murmured. 'Your trembling heart was my life. Fire ran in my veins at the touch of your soft fingers. Your eyes mirrored my heaven. Soul and body, body and soul, you stood between me and the night.' My voice sank smothered between my lips, and I knew I muttered to

myself. It seemed as if I watched her pale, pitiful
face and slight body from a great distance.   Her
soft tones ran murmurously on; but now the
trees buzzed in my ears, and the air, thick with
flitting Things, shut out the sight of her.   The
narrow way fled reeling from my vision into the
deep valley below.

'I ask no pardon,' I heard her cry, 'but one
thing only.'

She lifted her head, and her white face fronted
mine with a wild entreaty.

'I have dishonoured you and yours,' she said.
'I have no hope or future in this world.   There
is one thing only left me.   Give me that,' she
said, raising her clasped hands to me.   'Give me
that, you who are so strong and merciful.'

'Is it pity?' I asked, staring at her beseeching
eyes.

'Yes, pity,' she implored.   'Give me pity and
all that flows from pity.   Stand to me now in
the place of God, who has forsaken me, and give
me this one thing.   They said you were taken
with the fury of devils; they said you were relent-
less, mad with hate and the desire of vengeance.
But you are not.   They have spoken false of you,'
she cried.   'You are calm and still.   You look
down upon this thing and despise it—you are so
far above it—but you have no grudge against it.
You will deal nobly by it.   There are no petty
passions in your nature.   They told me you were

sworn to withhold from me freedom, to keep me in
the dust.   But you will not refuse this thing.   I
have put away from life all that is best and wisest,
all that is most gracious and worthiest ; I have
thrown immortality to the winds.   I am shipwrecked of all save this one thing—the piteous
pleasure of a wretched crawling worm.   Give
me this out of your nobility.   I pray to
you as to God, come not between us : give me
my freedom, and let me take up my miserable life
with *him*.'   .

'You put me in God's place,' I said.

'Yes, yes,' she said eagerly, 'in God's place.
You shall dispense mercy.   You shall pity.   I
want no pardon.   I am in the mire before you ;
let me live my lowly life.   I have but one passion,
but one thought, but one desire, but one hope,
and that is in him.   Do not keep me in chains.
Set me free that I may go to my bonds with him
and keep my paltry happiness secure.   See, I
tell you this, because you are my God.   You are
not upon my world ; you breathe a loftier air.
You have never loved me, a creature of such
vain clay.   Nothing could re-unite us two ; you
have no need of a dog at your heels to kick.   Let
me go out of your life.   You have no need of me.
Even had you loved me, you would not, you dare
not, have me back.'

She gasped her wild sentences in my ears, a
figure of forlorn entreaty ; and her face of beauty,

shining into mine, drove the black flecks from my sight, so that I beheld her suddenly the one being my of constant thoughts and prayers this twelvemonth.

'As God is my witness,' I cried to Heaven, 'I would take you out of Hell, though your soul were in black ashes.'

Her outstretched hands dropped a little; her wide eyes lowered ; and she shrank and shuddered from me in her fear. And by her drifted that Thing in the waving ferns. She fell upon her knees in the rough pathway and clasped my hand.

'You are my God,' she whispered. 'Give me this man.'

I shook her from me, and turned down the slope toward the black thicket.

'Vengeance,' said I, 'belongeth unto God.' I laughed. 'Go,' said I, 'I will give you this man.'

I could see her eyes gleam for a moment, as with a vivid joy; she made as though to follow me, but I moved to the very portals of the dark yews, and in a little she turned and went up the track. Pausing on the threshold of my downward way, I watched her white skirts creeping into the gloom ; and then I too turned and climbed down upon the village, leaving her to mount upwards to the downs, where lay that dread Thing waiting for her in the copse.

PHYLLIS

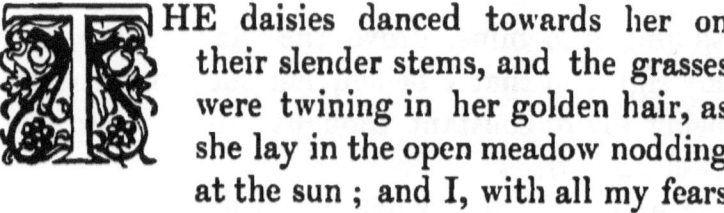HE daisies danced towards her on their slender stems, and the grasses were twining in her golden hair, as she lay in the open meadow nodding at the sun ; and I, with all my fears upon my face and a mad impulse in my heart, stole to her gently from the wicket. She stirred a little as I stayed beside her, stooping softly lower, and the small shadows of the sky fled in snatches across her sleeping face. At that moment, though her tremulous eyes are ever the light of my dim pathway, I dreaded lest they should open upon me and my shameful errand. So still she lay, dreaming like moonlight upon the fragrant bank, that I could have thought it but the eidolon of my love, so quietly recumbent. It seemed to me now as though Death, mistaken in his rounds, had come to the call of Sleep, and sat close, watching even as I. The cricket chirruped in the high summer noon, and bending nearer still I heard the long field rustling in a single wave, drowning her softer breath. Then,

as my lips dropped lower, came a still hush; the colour quickened in her cheeks to the race of my own desperate blood, and lifting her lashes she looked up at me.

I fell back in abasement with no words ready to my use, and starting she drew her lissom body to its full stature, gazing with surprise upon me at her feet.

'What did this mean?' she asked, her face suffusing swiftly with a delicate red.

'The sun,' I stammered, 'was too hot upon your face; and a spider——'

She swept from me with a gesture. 'I thought,' she said, 'at least you were a gentleman.'

'It has always been my intention to be such,' I murmured in reply.

'You have put off the experiment too long,' said she with much disdain.

'Do. you not think,' said I, rising, 'that in some circumstances gentility were Quixotic?'

'There is nothing more ultimate than honour,' she answered indignantly. 'It is an element in itself, and while our sex leans on yours you have plain duties.'

'I have thought of honour,' said I, 'but I find it a mere straw against you. We have plain duties,' I said; 'what rights have we?'

'You have,' she said, flashing at me, 'at least the right to your own company, as I to mine.'

She turned and made from me with the appearance of great dignity across the meadow slowly. I saw her moving for the wood in the full sunlight, her white skirts tossing over the grasses, her head erect and wonderful. At rest or in life *she* was my final law, not honour. Leaping from the bank I sped swiftly upon her. At my approach she paused and thrust her chin a trifle from me.

'I see, sir,' she said, with a quiver of her exquisite nostrils, 'that you will take no instruction upon the point of honour.'

'You forget,' said I, stilling my heart to be cool, and now timorous in her presence. 'There is but one passage from this field.'

'Perhaps, then, you will proceed, sir,' she replied, flinging her hand towards the wood.

'Nay,' said I boldly, 'I were better behind.'

'At a distance,' she cried quickly.

'At some distance,' I assented.

She bowed and went forward, and her fine grace caught away my breath, so that I stood gazing till she vanished through the wicket; then waking to find the heaven dark I rushed after her. The wood, obscurer at the outset, grew lighter as I advanced, and presently I saw her at a bend in the path picking her way over fallen branches. Hastening, I left so much space between us as suffered her to pass but rarely from my sight, and when an angle hid her I made upon her a few steps. Thus drawing through the brake we came out upon a clear, straight reach, down which I saw her flitting from the vista. And now the horrible remoteness of this passage was grown a dire torture to me, and with no thought but the one I bore down upon her speedily. Turning, she confronted me in an angry blaze, and my heart trembled at her warring eyes. The lips curled as they parted in scorn of me, but waveringly I broke in ere she spoke.

'I would have passed you,' I stuttered, 'being under the press of an engagement I had forgotten. But your hair—at the distance——'

She put her hand to her golden locks, and flushed at the touch.

'I thank you,' she said with some confusion. 'The grass has set it in disorder.'

At her embarrassment I was emboldened.

'It would have shortly fallen in a shower,' I explained with calmness.

'I am obliged to your courtesy,' she answered with her flush. 'It is not pleasant to pass for a spectacle.'

'I take some credit for my self-denial,' said I, 'for with that streaming gold before me this journey had been something more tolerable.'

'You are very good,' she murmured, and moved on, leaving me to gaze after her with wistful eyes.

There was no great stretch between us now,

and as I walked the rustle of her gown fell like
music on my ears.   And yet I was but commonly
happy.   When in the cold distance, it had
seemed life had no fairer prospect than to be a
little nearer; but now, grown familiar with the
neighbourhood, I desired another advance, chafing
at so frugal a pleasure.   At length my ardent
discontent provoked me past bearing.   I glanced
at the blue sky, the feathered elms, and the long
bracken.

'The year is mending,' said I.   'Nature is in
perfection.'

She made no immediate answer to my words,
but in a second half-turned her face upon the
level of her shoulders, making no pause.

'You should not have spoken,' she said.

I craved her pardon.   'The sense of com-
panionship,' said I, 'was so strong upon me that
I had forgot your presence was but of the body.'

She said nothing at the time, but in a little
looked back upon me as at a sudden thought.

'If this be so, you were better gone,' she said.
'There is also your pressing engagement.'

The echo of my own rash words struck me with
confusion, and I had no tongue to reply; but
soon she halted upon the path, and, stepping to
the side, motioned me on with a pretty gesture.

'You had then better pass,' said she gravely.

I stood for a moment close to her, and her
eyes—slow, quiet, and serious—met mine with

that intimate expression so dear to me. My
soul fused in the fire. 'I cannot pass,' I cried in
my fever. 'The devil keep engagements!'

'You speak in strong terms,' she answered, her
lashes falling for an instant over her eyes. 'It
is surely pitiful to see a grown man of this mind.
What keeps you back?'

'I had rather dwindle in your regard,' I said,
'than bulk beyond the horizon of your thoughts.
For the rest,' I cried, 'I have no reasons. As
well ask a grape for thorns as one that loves you
for reasons.'

'If you will not pass,' said she, 'at least
suffer me to do so,' and pushing by me she
resumed her way.

Though I had protested my desire of her company so bravely, eftsoon it came to be mere pain;
her economy of her presence fretted on my
nerves so dangerously that I was in despair lest
I should be incited to some fresh folly. To
see her was insufficient; I had the thought to
reach and touch her, and her continual grace was
beyond endurance. So when we were come to a
fork in the track sloping to the stream below, I
paused, on an impulse to end the hopeless fellowship.

'There is a short cut to the village,' said I;
'it will serve you best. I will rid you of myself.'

'I know it,' she answered, stopping also to look
at me quickly; 'I had determined upon it.'

I lifted my hat, and, swinging away, was going down the path, when I heard her voice.

'But 'tis a pity,' she said, 'to put you to this trouble. Why choose the longer? There is your engagement. I have no monopoly of this pathway.'

'The silence was too great for me,' I answered. 'We were easier apart.'

'You managed fairly,' she said gently. 'Do not thrust unkindness upon me.'

'I should perceive it to be only mercy,' said I; and, retracing my steps, followed her down into the narrow gorge.

A freshet ran swiftly through the bottom, and where the path fell from the steeps upon it, splitting upon an eyot of bracken, raced on each side about the white stones of a crossing. As she saw it she gave a little start, and glanced back at me.

'I did not remember,' she said in a troubled voice. 'There is no foot-rail here.'

'There are stepping-stones,' said I, 'to the islet and from the islet.'

She surveyed the crossing with a little alarm, and then, putting her foot to the verge, made as though to step upon the nearest stone. The spaces stretched wide between them.

'It shakes,' said she aghast.

'Pray let me be your aid,' said I.

'"Tis a man's work, and not a woman's,' she

said with some show of anger. 'The world is planned upon this principle of dependence.'

I leapt across the first space, and turning put out my hand to her.

'You must let me have your hand,' said I.

'It is unnecessary,' she answered. 'You have but to try the stages.'

'Your skirts!' said I; 'you must jump!'

'You may have my hand,' said she, and I pulled her safely to the stone.

But at that exquisite touch I was beside myself, and crossed to the next landing in a dream, my eyes upon her face, unconscious of the bubbles breaking in the eddies. And I saw, moreover, to my shame and to my glory, the golden hair loosening on the dainty head, menacing a sudden fall; while she all unawares stepped to me elegantly across the intervening straits. My mind was a mad whirlpool, my pulse beat as the fleet wings of a dove; and when she stood upon the eyot I flung myself at her feet in the bracken.

'Phyllis,' I cried, 'be with me always as upon this passage. The world is planned upon this principle of dependence, Phyllis.'

She started and turned pale and red.

'You have presumed too foolishly,' she said coldly; 'I had thought you were come to yourself. You cannot conceive how ridiculous is this position,' she said.

'Then,' said I, at the white heat of feeling, 'you shall find some other partner for the journey hence;' and, throwing myself upon the bracken, I folded my arms.

'You make a jest of my misfortunes,' she said icily. 'To choose this time were like you. I thank you for your past assistance.' And inclining her head she stepped to the further side of the eyot.

'Where are you going?' I asked.

'I will wade,' she answered curtly.

I laughed.

She hesitated, looking from the stony bed to her own sweet feet peeping from her gown.

'Some one will come this way,' she murmured.

'Once in a day,' said I, smiling.

She turned on me indignantly, and her eyes were daggers.

'You have no honour,' she said fiercely; 'I should have kept the wood between us.'

'It is true,' said I: 'you are my honour.'

'You have no honour,' she repeated with passion, and stamping her foot, brought down the golden hair in masses about her face. Rising, I fronted her swiftly, with a glowing heart, as she stood confused and flushing at the accident.

'Without you,' said I, murmuring low, 'I have no honour, Phyllis. I am desperate for lack of you; my brain is become an ingenious cheat for you; I am a rogue, a rascal, in your

presence. I know no deed I would not dare for
you. I would give my soul as I have given my
heart and life for you.'

My fervid eyes, drooping before her, beheld
but her dazzling gown swaying in the breath of
the valley.

'You were better, then, without me,' she made
answer lowly.

'That were the end,' I whispered.

The bracken, springing from my weight,
fidgeted in the silence till she spoke.

'You have surprised me most unfairly,' she
said softly; 'I was nearly come to tears.'

'I could have asked nothing dearer than your
tears,' said I; 'I had felt you were nearer to
me so.'

'What is it that you wish?' she asked, below
her breath.

I looked up, and found her gazing softly up
the valley. Her bosom came and went from me;
her lips were of quivering scarlet; her dishevelled
hair sparkled in the sunlight.

'I would take,' said I, 'what I would have
stolen this noon. I would touch your lips, my
sweet.'

'You may touch my lips,' she whispered.

 LAUGHED at her vivacious display of fear, and went a space further into the wood. I called to her, but she stood irresponsive on the white road. I retraced my way to the verge of the open, and took hold of her hand.

'Come,' I said, 'this superstition is ridiculous. You have gone this path many a time; it is the shortest track to the village.'

'It is Christmas Eve,' she returned with a nervous shiver.

'What of that?' I answered lightly. 'A wood is all one at Christmas or midsummer.'

She shook her head, but I could see she was plainly yielding to my persuasion.

'It was an ancient place of burial,' she said, 'where are still the disfigured bones of those that lived before Christ.'

'Every foot of green earth covers some decay,' I said. 'Come; the white road takes a tedious circuit into the valley.'

'They say,' she went on, and a thin tremble

ran in her voice—'they say that evil spirits take possession of this place on this night. They must vanish with the midnight bells for a twelvemonth ; on Christmas Eve alone are they abroad.

'I see,' I answered, laughing ; 'it is their protest against a Saviour. But come ; for the wind is rising, and a gale is growing on the moor.'

Her eyes shifted fearfully as she regarded me, and her skirts were fluttering in the fern. As she stood thus silent, there entered into my heart that fierce desire of her which had so long been beating about my soul. I snatched her hand, and, bending to her, held that wondering gaze with mine. A still peace stole into her face ; the warm blood trembled in her fingers ; I knew her for my captive, as she knew me for hers. We were thus for some short seconds, and then a sigh, as it were the distant voice of some encaged spirit, escaped her lips ; and my own mind followed the course of her thoughts. I loosened my grasp of her hand, but ere it fell from me a thrill started through her body, and the fingers closed upon mine with a little convulsive catch. In an instant an ecstasy had taken me, and she was swaying in my arms, passive and unafraid. The supreme delight of that moment touches me even now to the very quick of my being. I strained her to me, my voice murmuring words of endearment. She withdrew herself from me, watching my eyes with a troubled gaze.

'You will marry in this New Year,' she said earnestly. 'It is laid upon you. What would she think? You have your honour. You have been mad, and you have infected me with madness. It is the evil spirits of this field;' and she shuddered.

'I will be no slave to a preposterous notion of honour,' I cried. 'Is a man bound from his childhood? What our fathers have declared to us—shall we take that upon the mere statement? I have lived as a fool——'

'But you shall die as a man of honour,' she broke in upon my fervour.

'Rather,' said I, 'as a man of taste.' I took her into my arms again, and her reluctant body yielded to my strenuous passion.

'Remember,' she murmured. 'Ah, remember.'

'There is nothing irreparable,' I answered. 'All will wear a gay face in a week. She cares nothing for me; and I, even at this hour, have seen the folly of obedience. Your love has turned the stream of my life from a smooth and narrow channel. That is all. Better the contentment of two hearts than of a very giddy vanity.'

She made no sign, but it seemed to me that she surrendered herself to my pleading.

'We will take the track through the wood?' I said, caressing her.

'Yes,' she whispered faintly.

The grey clouds were flying in troops over the

moon, and the wind clapped boisterously about
our ears as we passed into the shelter of the pines.
Over the moor, which stretched solitary to the
black hills, it scudded and romped towards the
back parts of the valley; and as I turned upon
the very threshold of the wood it seemed as
though the plain was in the possession of many
roystering tenants—so much of stir and motion
was visible among the bracken and the gorse.
On the outset of the forest the straight columns
of the firs were creaking, but the inner recesses
lay hushed and dark, secluded in a shelving
bottom. I think that the noises of the fierce
wind, which blew with an icy breath, had restored
to her a sense of security; for though we might
not now be heard without shouting, she clung
restfully to my arm, and the short snatches of
light that blinked through the flying clouds revealed a soft and happy smile moving on her
face. As for myself, I had now my world, and
was become its veritable captain. The wood
roared in our ears; we slipped from the embrace
of the gale, and dropped down into the silent
close which had been the ancient sepulchre of
ancient peoples. And here a great change befell.
In the quiet of that place I could hear the wind
howling on the moor, and the sound of our footsteps struck harshly on the stillness. I had scant
room but for the one burning thought; yet for
a moment the strangeness of this unspeakable

stillness flashed through my mind, and I perceived
with an ignoble joy that her old fears were recur-
ring to her. She will press closer to me, I thought;
and was filled with an extravagant delight of her
touch. Suddenly, and when we were about the
heart of the thicket, little noises got up among
the dead leaves, and a thin whistling in the
skeleton branches. She clutched me in a quick
terror, and I soothed her gently.

'It is nothing, my love,' I said; 'the wind has
broken into the valley.'

'It is the graves,' she gasped. 'The spirits are
come out.'

She turned her face aslant towards the growing
noises, which appeared to creep along the ground;
the dead leaves hissed and slithered. Her body
bent across me, and her arms went round my
neck; but she held her eyes towards that crawling noise.

'Sweetheart,' I said, 'be brave.'

But on that instant a rushing fury filled the air,
and a great wind tore through the trees; vacancy
shrieked and moaned at us; and the gabble of a
thousand voices mocked us in the branches. In
my sight was nothing save the stirless wood and
the empty sky; in my ears were outrageous
sounds innumerable. At the first outset of
these strange presences she gave a low cry and
tightened upon me; and then a flash swept over
my eyes, and in that second her arms were ript

from my neck, and with a long wail of fear she
fled down the deep paths and vanished with the
noises into the wood.

When I returned to the full possession of
my wits I drew myself together and sped after her.
The way she had taken led over a heavy slope,
down which I was plunged into an infernal blackness where the underwood rose thick and sheer
upon all sides. Informed with a pricking dread
I called to her at the top of my voice, and clamours awoke in the gully; but I could see no sign
of her, and the copse was now as empty and as
silent as a churchyard under the moon. In this
desperate mood I ran along the track, crying to
the night without response, and presently burst
out upon the meadows that lay at the back of the
village. Here, too, all was silent, though the
wrack was racing in the sky, and the frosty lights
twinkled in the distant cottages. I had stood
irresolute and fearful for some minutes, the subject
of a rising horror, when there was a sudden crackle
of branches, and I saw her fleeting upon me out
of the dense brushwood. The apparition was so
abrupt that I momentarily started aback, but, as
quickly recovering, rushed to meet her with a
thrill of gladness. She made a weird figure in her
flight; her hair streaming at her back, her dress
disordered on her bosom, her hands clenching in
the air. She would have swung by me in her
panic, had I not arrested her with my arm. She

stayed, panting and wide-orbed, gazing at me with a distraught look, as it were of exultation.

'Sweetheart,' I said, 'you have been very foolish to allow this terror,' and made to take her in my arms.

She broke into laughter, murmurous and sweet, staring at me still from between her unblinking lids. The thought that came to me then was fraught with unspeakable horror, and I watched her in awe. The eyes shone spectrally on mine; the lips parted, as it seemed, in a mocking smile; and the dishevelled hair was curving and heaving in ragged waves on her head. Her face was the face of a mænad aflame. 'My heart,' I said, all agitation, 'be mine, be mine again. In the name of God,' I cried, 'close those eyes and come to me! Remember, we have been in love's land this night.'

'I remember,' she answered, and her voice rang shrilly in the air, 'that this night we have been with the dead.'

She threw herself back, and laughed, and I saw the tresses jigging on her head, screwing and whirling like the snakes in the head of a Medusa. Her laughter shook her, and, breaking from me she danced over the meadows into the night. And then I knew that the vulgar superstition of this place was true, and that the devils of the immemorial graveyard had crept into her hair and were gnawing at her brain.

That Christmas Day was a time of doubt and agony to me. I had no word of her whom I loved, and from her who was to be my wife came many weary messages. Impatiently between the thought of both I stood in the balance, unable to resolve my mind. My course had seemed plain before—plain and troublesome; to disengage myself from an arduous contract was clearer wisdom than to go shuffling through an unlovely marriage.

But now I could be sure of nothing, for she that had divorced me from my duty was in the possession of an Evil so gross as to withhold her humanity from her. And as the week wore on towards the New Year I was in no better case. Everywhere I heard of the visitation that had fallen upon her family, and all the countryside had pity on her. All day, I heard, she would keep the house, singing (they whispered) profane and hideous catches, the anxious care of her parents; but at nights, when the stars were full, she was abroad, riotous and mad, in the copses. The thought was too grievous for me, and I haunted the park at moonrise to get some more certain knowledge of her. On these excursions I saw her once, and the sight was pitiful and abhorrent. It was not that her awful tenants had robbed her of her beauty; that was unchanged—nay, rather raised to an unnatural glory by her madness. But to see her flying wildly through the trees, her large and mocking eyes sparkling under the stars, and the devils jigging in her hair, took me with such a sense of horror that I fled, ashamed and sick. She dangled an arm to me as she flashed past, tossing up her face and screaming at the sky. Thereafter I had no hope of her, but, schooling myself to the straight lines of duty, began with a poor heart to prepare against my wedding.

It was on the first day of the New Year that I was finally to resign from my dearest hope and open a fresh and uninspiring life with my cold bride. The thing had got thus far, and must reach the end. It was a bright, white morning (for the snow had fallen betimes) when I entered the little church, dumb to the fate arranged for me. As the service proceeded, the pitiable pretence, both of her and of myself, grew well-nigh intolerable, and I think never marriage has been imposed upon such indifferent auditors. But within a little of the end, and while we were yet upon the precincts of the altar, there came a sharp sound from the lower part of the church, and turning swiftly I perceived *her* coming up the aisle. She moved slowly, as though each step were made against an invisible resistance; her hair was twisting and coiling on her bare head; her wintry eyes were fastened upon me. I gave a short cry, but she took no notice, merely gazing from her wild and struggling eyes as she dragged herself towards the chancel. The church rose in a mutter of fear. I made a step to her. But at the chancel rails, and where the great Brazen Cross uplifts itself below the oriel windows, she fell suddenly to her knees. I watched her face. The devils jigged in her hair; it stirred gently, and then flowed soft and rich about her neck ; a shudder rushed through her; she hid her face in her hands. And when she raised it again, and her eyes sought mine, they were filled with a quiet smile of love, dewy with tears, and desolate with a sad and hopeless pain.

THE SWORD OF THE KADI

HAIDEE stole into her garden of roses and clung closely to me. There was a zephyr whispering in the myrtles, and the fragrance of a fine perfume on the gentle air; and I could not but think of it as the emanation of her divine presence. In her lissom body life ebbed and flowed in magnificent reversions as she pressed against my heart, and her lips quivered as I kissed her. She held me with her deep brown eyes, her head raised to regard me steadfastly.

'The Kadi has heard your call, my soul,' she whispered. 'He will send for you on the morrow.'

'Is it well?' I asked. 'What did he demand of me?'

'You are a Giaour,' said she; 'yet I love you; heart of mine, I love you,' she said passionately. 'What justice will the Kadi give when you meet upon the morrow? What justice?'

I bent to her slowly. 'My love,' said I, 'the Kadi shall not come between us twain. Though

he put mountains betwixt I will climb them;
though there be seas I will swim them; through
fire and sword I will pass unscathed—to thee.'

'He will put you to some trial,' she murmured.
'Pray God it be not too hard. He will put you
to some trial.'

I stooped, for I could barely catch her sweet,
low voice; and the fragrance passed through my
senses into my blood.

'I have sworn,' said I in that garden, 'he shall
come not between you, my beloved, and me.
Though his tests be fashioned in hell, I will shame
the Devil by my strength. I will be God in this
matter, and override the fiends themselves. Kadis
and all, they are impotent against the Giaour's
love. See, my Desire! To-morrow he shall give
justice to the world, and thee to me.'

I could see her mouth drawn at the verges, and
her olive cheeks pale in the soft moonlight. The
wind rushed out of the cypress grove and whistled
by us; she strained her face against mine, whispering in my ears.

'The Kadi is old, the Kadi is wise. Though
Allah himself should descend, He will avail nothing against the Kadi. There is the cunning of
years in this man. He has an evil eye; his face
is dark, as are his thoughts. He has pleasure in
the death of man; his desire is in the breaking of
hearts. Hell is his jest; Paradise is his scoff;
God is his scorn.'

'Star of my night,' I said to her, 'let his crafty wiles be infinite as the sands, I will be the sea to submerge them ; let his purposes be of the most desperate research, I will contend with them.   Have no fear for the morrow ; have only joy in this night, my love.'

She drew from me a pace, her large eyes beneath a film of tears.

'I have loved you, my beloved,' she said brokenly ; 'O my beloved, I have loved you. When you are come before the Kadi, think upon me.   Have me in your thoughts, my heart, as you are ever in mine.   And it shall haply befall that from before my image the enchantment of this devil shall flee.'

And vowing to her Prophet I would so hold her dear face in my mind, I watched her flit through the roses.

In the morning the Kadi called me into his presence about the hour of noon.   He lay upon his couch, white-bearded, pulling at his long pipe, and I entered before him with his slaves.

'My son,' said he, 'you have put upon me a heavy charge.   Were there not women as fair in your own land, that you would rob us of the pearl we cherish ?   Yet it is my place to deal justice with an even hand.   May Allah guide me !'

'This woman,' said I boldly, 'is dearer to me than any pearl.   Say if she shall not go whither she is held in most precious esteem ?'

'The Giaour,' said the Kadi, 'has no rights in
this world of ours. We give to him of our regard
for justice—nothing more. It is the Kadi's part
to hold the scales and judge between the good
and the evil.'

'My lord,' I cried, 'place me among the good,
for I would have this maid. Let nothing come
between me and her, between the Faithful and
the Giaour.'

The Kadi bowed his head. '·I have heard you,'
he said ; 'and I desire right and justice. Among
the Faithful Allah decides. You shall pass some
test for this girl.'

At his words I, suddenly recalling the anguished
whisper of Haidee, shivered for one moment where
I stood ; but on the next instant, recalling also
her sweet, low voice and dearest features, looked
him in the eyes and bowed after his own fashion.

'I will do this thing,' said I.

The Kadi clapped his hands, and from the
precincts of an inner room behind the silken hangings issued a slave, and put a table to the couch.

'What is love without faith and without discretion ?' said the Kadi. 'Nay, what also is it
without an imminent risk ? We purchase what
we value most at the peril of our lives,' said he.

'My life,' said I, 'is in the purchase of my
love.'

'It is well,' he answered; 'Allah shall decide,'
and, signing to his slave, bade him begone. 'He

that hath wisdom,' said the Kadi, ' and constancy
and courage, is meet for any bride, be she of the
Faithful or the Giaour. We have a game played
upon this table with six colours. It is for the
player to bring his colour through the moves into
the crowning square. There shall be given .you
six maidens bound each with a different colour.
The Giaour is crafty of the head. Choose you
the maiden, and if so be before the sun sets o'er
the Western Gate her colour shall stand upon the
crowning square, she shall depart with you, my
son. But if so be at sunset you have failed, upon
the Western Gate your head shall hang ere the
darkness be fallen. Allah shall decide, not human
frailty.'

Astounded at this strange pact, I turned upon
the table, whereon were many lines and colours ;
and as I gazed, reflecting upon my curious trial,
the hangings were swept apart and there entered
six fair women. Though her veil had fallen
across her face, I knew her by her gait and by
her trembling. Haidee slipped past me, a
scarlet band burning upon her sweet and delicate
arm.

' Life is a game from the beginning,' said the
Kadi. ' We are employed upon the puzzle many
years, and the sooner the end the simpler the
solution. The dead are fortunate. Choose you
the colour, my son. And forasmuch as the Kadi
holds the balance in his hands, keep counsel with

yourself. But in the end you must tell me your
choice. They are all fair women, not one alone,
my son; yet you may depart if you have now the
mind.

But looking at Haidee in the centre of her
fellows, her face paling as she opened her dewy
eyes upon me with affright, I turned to him and
said :

'My lord, I will do this thing.'

She had prayed me to keep her picture in my
thoughts; but now her dear presence filled my
soul. The Kadi turned to his pipe again, while
I, with my eyes upon the scarlet about her arm,
fell to my work with a heart of fire.

* * * * * *

From the high noon the sun declined upon the
city gate, but my task was unfulfilled. One by
one in the order of their moves had I placed
those pieces in their squares, placed and replaced,
moved and removed, adjusted, readjusted, schemed,
manœuvred, calculated, and contrived—but in
the end it was all one : no nearer came the scarlet
to my haven of desire. My brain whirled and
was weary; the colours ran in my eyes; each but
the one that blazed in my vision came within
reach of my goal, but I thrust them back—
unashamed and reckless. And as the sun fell
lower the Kadi lifted his eyes from the board and
beckoned, and the room filled with slaves; and
behind them was one taller than the habit of

their stature, bearing a great sword. Raising my
face from the darkening room I glanced through
the archway and beheld the dome of the Western
Gate, as scarlet in the sunset as the ribbon upon
the naked arm of my beloved.

'There is yet one half-hour, my son,' said the
Kadi.

The faces of the maidens wore a marvelling
look, but all was silent in that room. Dazed with
the play and my long solicitude, I let my gaze go
round them. Foremost of them all was one, tall,
most fair with flowing locks, with a great deli-
cateness of air, bound round with a blue band
that did her infinite service. And it seemed to
me, as I gazed at her, that there lurked in her
blue eyes a melting humour to seduce the soul of
man from the straight way of honour. So out of
keeping was it with that time that involuntarily
I swept round and found Haidee's great eyes of
brown fastened upon me utterly. Her bosom
quickened with her breathing, and beneath the
soft orbs of those great eyes I could see the soul
couchant, chained only by a woman's fear.
With a cry I fell into my work again.

The Kadi took the long pipe from his mouth and
stroked his beard. The pieces straggled upon my
board, and on the margin of the crowning square
gleamed the blue; behind showed the scarlet
infinitely removed. I looked up, and once more
the blue eyes gazed into my face; they were soft

and roguish as the twinkling sea, but the eyes of
Haidee were as the gazelle. I turned upon my
love, backward, alas! in the cold distance; but a
little stood betwixt me and doom. I felt the
slaves draw nearer from behind; the Kadi stroked
his beard. Haidee's lustrous eyes leapt out upon
me in fear and passionate love, as she leaned to
me nearer from her place; but the mist was in
mine, and the blue eyes smiled at me through
the haze, the white arm gleamed in the falling
sunlight. Haidee was in the dusk.

A sudden stir rose in the room; the Kadi
moved slightly; and I was aware of the great
sword turned to the red of blood above me. My
flesh crept upon my body in the silence. I put my
fingers to the blue piece upon the board and
thrust it forward: I saw Haidee's soul burst its
bonds and leap forth; the sunlight faded swiftly;
I reached out my hand and laid it upon a warm,
palpitating bosom.

'O Kadi,' I cried, throbbing, 'the blue was
my choice.'

The Kadi smiled.

 LEFT the ship at the nearest port and went direct to London with my mind full of her. It was odd that throughout my long absence I had thought of her but little (the life had been crowded with distractions), and yet as I drew home her face came nearest from the past, remitting the vivid impressions of my voyage into an obscure background. It was her eyes I watched in the blue waves; her frown clouded the skies; her smile danced in the ripples. To love her was no shame, I thought, though to proclaim that love had been dishonour. The touch of that land that contained her gracious body thrilled me as no fervour for my country had been able; to stand upon English soil was to be within the precincts of her worship. The folly blazed in my blood; I could no more withhold myself than my thoughts; hot-foot I drew into the town, with my unruly fever in my eyes. I meant no harm; I had even an inner joy of self-sacrifice; to see her was to put me to a new

martyrdom, and yet I had pleasure in my torture.
The Day of Judgment could not have stayed me
from her. She had slipped out of my hands long
since, but I was mad enough to take delight, as
it were, in a dream of visiting her face anew; I
should see once more the lines of intimate grace
I carried in my soul, and, masking my memory,
go strutting upon my stilts into a wonderful
vainglory. She had never been nearer me than
now, remote as she was by three wild years of
wandering.

She stood with one foot upon the fender as I
entered, her forehead bent upon an open hand,
and, as it seemed to me, her face had been worn
with tears. But at my approach, starting from
her abstraction, she took a step or two to meet
me, held out her hand, and gave me her gayest
welcome.

'You!' she said: 'you! Heaven grant us
these surprises! I had thought you in Japan, in
Patagonia, in Manicaland.' A little trembling
laugh broke from her. 'What brings you here?
Is it peace, or is it war?' And she turned
swiftly to the fire again.

She had, I thought, run through a dozen
moods in the greeting; and, acquainted as I was
with her fickle habit of mind, the transition
puzzled me. She was white to the verge of her
red lips.

'I am straight from the ship,' I told her. 'I

came out of a desire——well, we have been old
friends, and three years is a long track in a man's
life.'

I laughed myself; but it was a laugh betwixt
pleasure in her presence and fear of my own
actions. At the moment I felt I was best at a
distance.

'You have not called at your club?' said she
slowly.

'No,' said I, in wonder at her tone.

She smiled, and dropped into a chair with her
individual grace. With her eyes she bade me
sit, and leaning to me stared gaily in my face.

'No,' said she, 'three years—is it?—have left
no mark on you. You were always handsome,'
she said roguishly.

'And you,' I answered, catching her airy
manner—'you are as God made you: not a shade
less lovely.'

She put her head back with her old gesture;
her eyes danced.

'You would have done much for me once,' she
said archly.

'Not once,' said I simply.

Her eyes dropped; her face shadowed; she
rose and moved slowly to the window by which
the street was roaring. Something in her gait
struck me as most desolate. She stood drumming
her fingers on the pane, and watching the traffic
without attention. I too rose and followed her.

'I had forgotten,' I said : 'I should have asked
you. I have been out of touch with life. I have
heard nothing.' She turned upon me eyes of sudden terror. 'Your husband is living?' I asked.

She passed her hand over her brow. 'O yes,'
said she ; 'he is living.'

Her misery went through me like a knife ; I
was within reach of her golden hair, upon which
the sunlight rested. Had I met her gaze I think
I should have taken her in my arms ; as it was, I
could not keep my passion out of my voice.

'But yourself,' I murmured, 'yourself, dear :
you are happy? There is nothing to regret?'

She sighed and tossed her head. 'O no,' said
she with a show of petulance ; 'what should there
be, my dear stranger?' She walked back to her
seat with an indifferent air. 'Come,' she went
on more pleasantly, when we were seated again,
'tell me of your doings. The world has not
stood still for you, I suppose.'

My tongue was clumsy enough in her company, but I traversed with her my adventures in
rude places. She heard me, smiling with her
eyes, put in a question to exhibit me her interest,
laughed with me at my dragoman's extrava-
gances, stared in distressful sympathy with my
dangers ; and presently, as though with a slow
ebbing of her curiosity, drew off into a silent
reticence from which my greatest sensations
might not disturb her. She sat back in her

G

lounge, regarding me with tacit, restless eyes, as if my voice were merely the chatter of a phantom; and ever and anon would start, and, clutching at the arms of her chair, glance to the window with a scared face. The comedy, if such it was, had no attraction for me. My narrative lost heart, my tongue halted; she came out of herself and looked at me piteously. I was unable to refrain my pardon; I smiled, and dipping into my pocket drew forth a string of pearls and dangled them before her. She brightened at the sight, and catching them in her hands appraised their beauty.

'Of your own fishing?' she asked prettily.

I nodded. 'They fit with your white neck,' I said.

Her glance fell shyly upon me; she threw them round her throat, rose, and, turning to the mirror over the mantel, laughed and looked at me.

'Once,' said she, smiling, 'these would have been for me.'

'Not once,' I murmured—a second time that day. I strove to move my eyes from her, fearful what they might reveal; but, meeting hers, I saw therein a strange look that set the pulses beating in my body. Her cheeks were drawn as with pain, but her full orbs seemed to yearn towards me. My voice trembled.

'They are yours,' I said; 'I have loved you, as you know, for years.'

Suddenly she sprang to me, and put her arms about me.

'Take me away,' she cried, 'take me away. Let me go with you. Take me away!' and her weeping face was lifted to mine in a passion of entreaty.

The thing passed in a flash. I had scarce realised her arms were round me (so staggered was I by her movement) when she was gone from me, and leaned against the fireplace sobbing. I leapt to her; she stepped aside and burst into laughter.

'I was born for the stage,' she said. 'My dear traveller, was it not wonderful? What did you think? Don't speak of proprieties,' she cried, waving her hand fantastically, and showing her white teeth in her laughter: 'I know they were round your neck. But it is art—it is art;' and her merriment rang through the room. She finished with a little gasp that left her red mouth open.

I had not recovered from my wonder, and my heart ached with bitterness. I took my hat and moved towards the door.

'I am sorry,' I said, and my voice was low— 'I am sorry not to have played up to you more worthily. I have the misfortune to feel and not to simulate. On the stage I had been useless save in loving you.' I paused near the door. 'Forgive my sincerity,' I said.

'Are you going?' she asked indifferently. My answer was to turn the handle; for my limbs were trembling with the stress of that interview. Suddenly she was beside me, her back against the door.

'You shall not go,' she panted. 'I will not have you go. Stay! Stay!' she pleaded earnestly. 'You do not understand. I will tell you—I will tell you,' she gasped. 'You think me mad. You shall know this afternoon.'

I could not doubt the reality of her emotion. I turned and went back; and for a time neither of us spoke.

'You think me mad,' she repeated presently, as though the silence were too much for her. 'I could not bear you to leave me;' and, with a little hysterical laugh, 'yours is not the only neck I have clasped,' she said.

Utterly bewildered at the remarkable turn in our intercourse, I went mechanically to the window without reply. In an instant the street filled with howling news-boys. There was a sharp cry; I felt a hand on my shoulder, and, turning, found her white face near me.

'Come to the fire,' she whispered hoarsely. 'Don't stay here. Come to the fire.'

I was so lost in my amazement that I could do nothing but obey her, and was on the point of moving, when as quickly she stopped me.

'No, no,' she said. 'I have no right. You

shall know. The window,' she cried; 'the news-
boys ! It is all come at last,' and buried her face
in her hands.

I looked out into the street. The tide ran full
along the roadway; cabs rattled and carts rolled;
a flowing stream of passengers went by. A boy
flashed into sight, and paused, trailing a news-
bill. There was a deathly quiet in the room;
then suddenly I turned, stricken with a sickly
dread. Her eyes were upon me as the eyes of
a hunted creature; she crouched in her chair; a
sob broke from her.

'I said you should know,' she whispered, so
lowly that I could barely hear her.

'It is you ?' I asked, and scarce knew my own
voice. The dishonour of this fair woman so
publicly proclaimed touched me to the quick.
She made no answer. The frail body seemed to
shrink, looked wan and pitiful; the white bosom
rose and fell in a tumult; the eyes were wide
and wild upon me. 'What is this you have
done?' I cried.

'Had it been for you——' she whispered.

'My God!' I said. Her words choked back
my scorn and indignation. Had it been for me
she had sinned, I had forgiven her for her great
temptation.

'I was so lonely,' she whispered. 'He left me
to myself, used me unkindly. One must have
distractions. You too had forsaken me, and

were half the world away. The Devil tempted me, not love.'

I held my peace.

'My God!' she cried, 'I have had no love but for you.'

'This man——?' I said.

'I hate him,' she flashed forth; 'oh, I hate him.'

At that moment the door opened. I know not what instinct proclaimed to me his identity, and at this point of time I can hardly recall the exact sequence of the next events. But in that instant I knew him. Her face, with its craven fear and hatred, shrank from him. He made towards her, not noticing my presence. With her eyes she repulsed him, but he only grinned.

'The Devil take these lawyers,' said he. 'My dear, we have crossed the Rubicon, as you may know from the streets. Let us make as comfortable a bargain as possible.'

Her eyes burned; her voice rebelled in her throat; she leaned away spasmodically. A thousand times had those lustrous eyes, that graceful form, that dainty head, risen into my mind and dwelt in my dreams. And now she lay there pitiful and shrunken, her lovely face aghast with the horror of this approach, mutely calling for protection, so humble, so hopeless, and so lovely still. Something rose within me and surged into my throat; my brain went round in a whirl and settled. I strode out of my corner into the light.

'Sir,' said I, 'whatever is your business with this lady, it shall be with me, who am her future husband.'

HERE had never been the slightest question as to their relations. I had indeed fallen at one time into the common folly of the lover, and nursed a bitter jealousy of him, but after the passage of this madness the merest observation had been sufficient to re-assure me. It is true he was unmarried, and had many qualities that take a woman, but I believe he was really quite indifferent to the sex save as the source of some amusing friends. He was very sober and good-natured, and had a lazy regard for every one that came within his acquaintance. The two had grown up in the same countryside, and were on terms of unusual intimacy. She considered him a man of the world, which he was beyond question, and assumed him as a person of profound knowledge, which as certainly he was not. These opinions, with those early associations, were the credentials upon which she assigned him the position of her guide and counsellor. He was no doubt an excellent fellow, · sufficiently

wise; but from the moment of my infatuation
I viewed his easy access to her with much chagrin
and envy.   So close a proximity was denied me,
though I made the most desperate efforts to
obtain her confidence.   It seemed that I was
never to persuade her of her affection for me.   In
the privacy of my own thoughts I had long
since resolved upon the state of her heart.   Many
signs pointed at her condition ; for one thing
she had come to betray a blushing embarrassment if we met of a sudden, and though she
was able to recover pretty quickly, after the
manner of women, yet her eyes would still hold
their trouble for some little time, as though her
nature were but slowly settling from its dis-
turbance.   Indeed she was herself most uncertain
of her mind, and sometimes I thought I had
detected in her little airs of conduct a fear of
her own bewilderment.   She was new to the
sensations, and avoided considering them with an
instinct something between awe and shame.   I
think if she had found the courage to confront
herself boldly she would have confessed to an
attachment for me, would at least have realised
in what current she was drifting, even if she did
not acknowledge it openly.   But hitherto her
heart had been absolutely virginal, and to find
it suddenly active with strange feelings was to
throw her into a confusion she could not understand.   Her soul was so private and so dainty

that the presence therein of a new and foreign
interest set her quivering with maidenly alarm ;
she fled from the thought and memory of it,
but there it was, still awaiting her on her return, a veiled and silent mystery she would not
examine. It was this doubt drove her back
upon her established companion, not for advice
indeed, but as a familiar landmark with which
she need have no scruples.

My passion was very manifest, and I was
aware he watched it, as it were, out of his
sleepy eyes. I did not mind that the world should
observe it, if only it were from a little distance ;
but that he, so close a neighbour of her own,
so intimate an environment of our two selves,
should be the witness of my uneven passage to
her heart, chafed me beyond endurance. I believe he was so indifferent to her beauty that
it was a quiet amusement for him to note the
love of others for her. Of all these I was
assuredly the most in her thoughts, and yet she
held me at a greater distance than any, while
he looked on with his smile. He was privileged
with opportunities of sight and touch of her,
which were nothing to him, but would have
been all the world to me. Had he been her
brother, their close friendship would not have
annoyed me ; but there he was, unperturbed, in
serene possession, so to say, with the most obvious
and irresistible chances to his hand—and not a

natural tie between them. It is true he was never impertinent in his observance, never by a word gave me a hint of his knowledge; but his eyes followed me in the course of my passion; and it irked me to remark the intelligent regard with which he met me.

It will seem odd, but I had never put her to the ultimate test by a profession of my love. To say the truth, I still feared her own terror, and was unwilling to risk my hopes prematurely, ere she had been induced to recognise her feelings. But with my eyes, with every act and service of my life, I invited her to my heart, and to the urgency of my silent pleading I knew she must yield.   Only this one irritation stood between me and content; and it was recurrent day by day in all the trivial facts of our intercourse.   Once I had a rose for her from my garden.   She took it with uncertain fingers and a precipitate flush, and carried it instantly to her bosom.   It lay in a coign of that sweet bodice, and I knew she had given herself tremulously to the delight of that moment.   It flashed upon me then that I had at last got to my end, and a vision of this exquisite surrender dazzled my mind with its surprising lights.   I seemed to see the sacred soul come creeping softly from its pinnacle of virgin majesty down to the very level of my eyes, at last to inspect and welcome this strange love. And then, almost as I would have spoken, he came out from his midday rest, whistling an air and scrutinising the signs of the sky with amiable carelessness. The smoke was wreathing from his cigarette, and his friendly glance ran down her faultless figure with approval. It rested for a moment on the rose; then shot silently at my face. He put his cigarette between his lips again; said the rain was gathering, yawned and passed on. But the light had faded out of her eyes; she contemplated his miserable clouds; her voice rang coldly; she was itching to be off; she turned, and the rose fell from her bosom. You will not wonder that the grotesque situation filled me with indignation. She would pace the walks with him in the morning for an hour together, while I went solitary; she listened to his desultory talk as though it were the wisdom of centuries. She was uncertain of a strange course if she had not his opinion on it, and at the moment when she seemed to be yielding to the rarest emotions of her nature, his shadow had sufficed to frighten her from the trembling surrender.

It was impossible to remain in this distressing uncertainty. I loved her in a tumultuous fashion and the tide of my passion might not be unduly retarded. I must put her to the test, I found, and dare my dismissal. All fortunes must come to the touch at last, I thought, and I had a lively faith in my own success. When I had

reached the resolution my heart mounted like
a lark, as I set out that day upon my adventure.
I found her murmuring an air to her own playing in the twilight of the drawing-room.   She
rose on my entrance and bade me welcome with
some show of diffidence, as I fancied.   Perhaps
my intention glowed in my eyes.   She remarked
upon the softness of the night, and pushed open
the long window that overlooked the lawn.   There
she stood with the melancholy light touching her
white neck, with the breeze stirring her rich hair.
She looked very young and very pure, and a little
embarrassed.   At the vision she presented of
troubled innocence I was half in the mind to
keep my words unsaid yet a little longer, to go
forth from her and leave her still unacquainted
with passion, with that mystery still veiled, still
fearful of the voices that whispered within her.
To rob her of those doubts and tremors seemed
for that moment to reduce her to the horrid
prose of life; she stood now on heights romantical, with strange and mystic regions about her
feet.   But this fancy passed like a shadow over
my determination, and when, startled at the long
silence, she turned and glanced wistfully at my
face, I made a movement forward and took her
hand.

' Dearest,' said I, ' I love you.'

She shrank from me against the window; her
eyes were beggars for my mercy; but heedless in

the full course of my passion I discovered to her
my hopes in a flood of language. She had said
never a word, but her eyes had fallen, and the
hand she would at first have wrested from me lay
still and hot in mine. Even when I paused in
my entreaties she made no answer.

'My darling,' I pleaded, 'you love me? Give
me some word, sweetheart. Give me your eyes
and I will read it there.'

She shook her head, all atremble from head to
foot.

'No,' she murmured brokenly, 'I cannot. I
don't know. To-morrow—no—I will write to
you. It is better. Not to-day. I am—you
have startled me.'

With that, and one look of her pitiful eyes, she
slipped from my hold and vanished into the
garden. I stood for a while wrestling with the
temptation to pursue her, but at length regaining
possession of myself left the house glowing with
elation. She loved me beyond question.

All the next day I had no word from her,
and refrained from the house with the greatest
difficulty; and when on the following day there
came no letter I fell from an elevation of joyous
confidence into critical misgivings. I took to
strolling in the vicinity of the house I might not
enter, and here in the afternoon befel that which
once more filled me with the fiercest chagrin.
When I espied him entering at the gate there

revived in me all the foolish jealousy of my
early acquaintance with them.   He then had
the liberty of those precincts from which I was
an exile.   Him she would meet with smiles,
while from me she had fled as from a danger.   In
my fancy I could hear her merriment as they
laughed together ; and I not there to intercede
against her gaiety.   I hung about in concealment
in the humour of a desperado, and when, at the
end of an hour he came out, her voice accom-
panied him to the foot of the walk.   I heard her
thank him with some perturbation ; and when he
left the gate, across his face a smile broke slowly,
and he chuckled to himself.   Then in the fury of
this sudden revelation I could have followed and
struck him to the ground.   For now the object of
his visit had flashed upon me in an instant : she
had distrusted the evidence of her own perplexed
feelings and had fallen back upon his cooler judgment.   Upon his verdict was to hang my fate ;
he was the recipient of my confession ; to him I
had poured out my hopes ; his was the decision
that should make or mar my happiness.   The
more I reflected upon this turn in events the more
embittered I became.   This was not the act of
one who truly loved me ; a sincere devotion should
be held in confidence ; that another should be
summoned to review the delicate characters of
love was repulsive to its divine instinct.   Even
though she had veiled her problem in impersonal

hypotheses it were an affront upon the sovereignty
and independence of the passion.   He was called
in to pronounce upon the case, as it were, and
from him I was to take my fortune.   The thought
broke like gall in my stomach.   I had no doubt
now that I should have her answer at once ;
and so it fell out, for that evening she wrote
to accept me.   It appeared then that he had
' passed ' me, and I might breathe with freedom.
The idea was so ludicrous that I screamed with
laughter, which lapsed, however, into a sudden
angry oath.   To go through our joint lives on
these terms was impossible.   One long farce
would be daily in progress by our fireside if
she were never to be weaned from this dependence.   A dictator betwixt me and her actions !   I vow I was in love to desperation, yet
such a marriage was preposterous, and I took
my pen to disentangle myself from the false
position.

My face must have glowered on him as dark as
night when he entered, but he nodded affably and
lolled in an arm-chair.   I could not trust myself
to speak, but my silence did not affect his complacency.   He smoked and talked with benevolent
lethargy.

No one had seen me these last few days.   Had
I been ill or away ? he inquired.   And then my
my wrath broke out before his imperturbable
smile.

'Neither the one nor the other,' I answered, 'merely patenting a scheme to suppress meddlers.'

'Ah!' he said lazily, 'good.'

'See here,' I said, 'I want no interference in my affairs. I can put my own fingers in my fortune, and when I've need of yours I'll ask for them. This letter,' and I waved it at him, 'was written to your dictation. I would sooner have got it from the Devil.'

He lifted his eyebrows, but made no sign of discomfort.

'Advice is cheap enough,' he said, 'nor am I likely to give mine where it isn't solicited. Of course I regret your annoyance, but it's only natural. If I am asked—' he smiled and shrugged his shoulders, 'well, what am I to say?'

'I'm not going to take any favours from you,' I burst forth, 'I'll not owe you any thanks.'

'Thanks!' said he, smiling; 'scarcely thanks, is it?'

'She should never have come into our quarrel, but in my passion I had lost my manners.'

'I will not accept her at your hands,' I said. 'If she will not have me of her own free will, she'll not of yours; and that's my answer.'

'Have you!' he cried, starting to his feet, and betraying for the first time a lively excitement. 'She'll have you then, after all? Good Lord, I'd no notion of this,' and catching up his hat in an absent manner he left the room.

I stood for a moment in silent bewilderment, and then as the meaning of his conduct grew upon me, some bar fell from my heart, and a flood of delicious feeling swept along all my nerves. I tore my letter into shreds.

DICK A-DYING

H E lay upon his rough bed, confined within meagre wrappings, and contemplated the mangy ceiling. In one corner a spider wandered about its dusty web; the plaster, distempered with the grime of smoke, was streaked and patched with blots of darkness; it gaped with swelling fissures, from which thin filaments hung, and shook at the rumble of passing vehicles. The low roof stretched overhead as a particoloured map, in which his eye travelled listlessly over seas and continents. He had the distribution of the elements by heart, and could have redrawn them in their proper proportions. The squalid ceiling held no more for him now than the circumjacent space within the four walls, than the dingy street at which his attic window blinked. The phenomena of that room were worn smooth by long use; yet the day had its own slow history. In fine weather the autumnal sun struck through the panes at high noon, and fell on the ragged carpet. There the thread of

light lay inert and dead for some time, then
stirred sluggishly and crept towards the doorway.
His eyes were wont to watch it till it vanished
somewhere through the chinks, along the wall
and into the street again. Towards evening it
flashed on the windows across the way, and was
then gone from his cramped world altogether.
The fall of night on these occasions was an agree-
able event, for it was as though more incidents
attended the close of day. There was constantly
some change in his purview. The air turned
chilly; the sky showed some faint reflections from
the west; the mists rolled out of the river; and
lights sprang up in the houses opposite. At that
time, too, the streets emptied of its yelling
children; doors clapped-to behind home-comers:
a piano tinkled in the distance; an early tippler
beguiled the way with song; and as the candle
spluttered out by his bedside, Dick drew nearer
to sleep.

The day broke bleakly, and for the more part
in fog or rain. Perched in his high seclusion, he
could despatch his gaze across a wide stretch
of housetops, broken by peaks and chimneys.
Narrow rims and gutters in the prospect marked
the deep streets and lanes that cut this monstrous plateau into islands. It seemed to him as
though he on his heights were the single tenant
of a silent and desert world, reaching indeter-
minately away, with stack on stack of smoking

chimneys, and wave on wave of rolling gables.
Below ran an invisible life in which he might take
no part; monotonous, it would appear from the
unchanging sounds of traffic and communion, but
still a world too familiar to be forsaken for this
motionless and quiet sphere above. This thought
had grown clearer in him, had mounted into a
constant pain. He supposed he should be gone
from this outer life in a little without the liberty
of farewell; and he was kept still within hearing
of it, a parcel of the next, to which he had not
yet resigned himself. By this he had grown too
weak for movement, though the throes of his
malady had left him; and his mind, revolving in
itself, was free to regard the prospect with its
best fortitude. As he approached death he must
fit his spirit for the dissolution : must, at least,
withdraw it from the interests of the street, lest
it should take its separation too desperately at
the moment of departure. To think upon that
packed life, its marvellous passions, its snug
corners, its spacious breadth and singular continuity, the very chequers in its ample warmth
and brightness—to take all this into his thoughts
in a flash, and to forecast his good-byes, chilled
his heart to an extremity of cold. He was upon
the precipice, with his eyes full-opened on the
fall; and the agony of that anticipated descent
appalled him. It were better, he concluded, to
watch the yellow sunlight, to travel with the

the spider to and from his slimy web, to count the stacks upon the houses in his superior world, rather than to suffer his soul to dwell in this torment. When these distractions failed he would have the refuge of sleep, upon which his worn body declined now with increasing readiness.

As he lay upon his pallet the door opened noiselessly, and a man stood within the precincts of the room and regarded him. Dick turned his head and smiled as at a familiar face.

'A little weaker,' said the doctor, taking hold upon the thin wrist. 'You have had a constitution of steel.'

Dick looked at him. He was a man of some sixty years, meanly dressed; his moustache powdered yellow with the use of snuff, his eyes hard and weary, his shoulders stooped, his skin fitted tightly over a bony skull. He met his patient's eyes, and passed them without recognition; he had, no doubt, some grave point of treatment to discuss with himself, and could not be at the bother of ceremony. This man had looked into the eyes of death for forty years; and yet (Dick wondered) did he spare a little pity for this one of many thousands? The doctor hummed a gentle air; he sat upon the mattress, scanning the sick man.

'It is a spurious kindness to keep the truth from you,' said he.

Dick nodded; his eyes were fastened on the

other's features. He hardly heard. His career
had been brief, as careers go ; he had made and
lost it for himself; for fifteen years he had been
in the enjoyment of vain pleasures. He had been
at pains to constitute a scheme after his own
taste ; he had taken the trouble to step out of
his native circle into another he conceived of
greater opportunity and promise. He had given
no thought to enduring friendships ; he had
married no wife ; he had spent upon himself the
years of his manhood. This doctor alone of all
men that had fallen within the compass of his
acquaintance was to compassionate him on his end.

The doctor took some snuff.

' Have you no friends ?' he asked.

' I have a brother,' said Dick.

' Send for him,' replied his visitor.

Dick's glance drifted to the window. The
street was roaring with the midday voices ; the
air hung heavy with smoke and mist. At a
motion the dirty attic and its contiguous squalor
had lost their proximity, and he was regarding
himself with the eyes of childhood. The vices
and pleasures of his adult life invited him vainly
from their cold distance. In the full costume of
manhood, though the frame of it was shrunken,
with the complete experiences of his five-and-
thirty years, he had now the vision and emotions
of a boy. The habit of manliness, like the
pleasant vices, had faded inconceivably ; the

ghost of a strong will, bloodless and frail, stared
wofully through its prison-bars. The spirit lay
a-dying with the flesh, leaving vivid only the sense
of horror and the faculty of tears. Thrills of a
soft affection stirred along his nerves, and gentle
voices were calling in his ears. It was strange
how he could resume those preterite feelings,
upon which his memory had made no call for
years which he had long since flung off as attach-
ments unworthy of the larger mind. He could
not, indeed, perfectly reconstruct the ancient
company of his childhood: for of the faces many
came as shadows, some from the grave, some
from oversea; with variable traits and uncertain
features. But their memories crept very near
him, enclosing him in a warm gush of affection;
and closest and warmest of all was that figure
of his brother, now the sole relic from his school-
days, wearing the gracious air of common associations and claiming the tie of blood. If his eyes
must shut upon the world, let it be with something familiar in that final gaze.

'I should like him to be here,' said he in his
thin voice.

'I will telegraph,' said the doctor.

There seemed that afternoon a pause in the
course of the sun. It was but a trickle of light
that dribbled through the shallow mist, but it
was long in passing. As the hours wore on,
Dick could hear mounting from below snatches

of sound in the house : as each rose he stiffened
in his bed with an anxious expectancy, his mouth
ready seamed for a smile. Betweenwhiles his
thoughts flowed in a sluggish dream, wherein the
past was very clear and present. But at the
fall of night the doctor returned, a brown
envelope between his fingers. Dick rose upon
an elbow painfully and searched the passive face.
Some change there in the narrow eyes answered
his silent question ; he sank again.

' He is sorry ; he has a great press of business,'
quoth the doctor.

At the words those amiable phantoms of boy-
hood departed from their neighbourhood, and
resumed their proper distance. The past fell
clean out of sight, and but the present filled the
room. Yet the yearning for this familiar object
wherefrom to close the eyes survived from the
barren experiment. His associates were gone out
of his life ; he had quarrelled upon a woman with
one, had betrayed the honour of another, was
forgotten of a third. In this way and in that
he had destroyed an environment of no particular
consistency. There seemed to him left now only
the bare walls of his material enclosure. There
was a girl to whom he had professed more than
the current affection ; and perhaps she, too, had
taken him at a superior value. But these attach-
ments were of the whim, too casual, too ordinary,
too multitudinous for grave issues. His fancy

lingered for one instant on this careless creature of black eyes, but the next perceived her wincing through her paint, and withdrawing her dainty skirts from the contact of his tawdry bed. The incongruous apparition fled at the glimpse, and he beheld the doctor regarding him with lowered eyes.

'There is no one else?' he asked.

Dick saw his spider nesting for the night; in the candle-light black shadows dodged and flickered over the ceiling; the smoke floated up as incense; and little draughts whistled in the cracks of the floor. The doctor rose, and pulled the blind across the window. The action had a touch of homeliness, and carried with it suggestions of a fireside. He was shutting out the dark from this poor candle, and would turn to talk with him. Dick would fetch topics even now out of his manifold experiences, with which they might beguile the remaining hours. He would discuss with abating breath stray ideas from his rich memories, and make, as it were, a final stand in life. Death should approach unheard in this last exchange of sympathies. Or at least he should sink quietly into oblivion, with some one watching who had done him kindly offices, and had some sense of those agonies which he was to endure.

'Doctor,' said he; 'have you seen many die?' His gaze moved wistfully over the parched face. The doctor shrugged his shoulders.

'I have lived some sixty years,' said he; 'and my own death will be at the tail of very many.'

Dick's eyelids drooped. Life, then, was so mortal to this man that its termination must be but an unessential incident, so slight and common as to pass without record in the memory. To die with those sharp, expert eyes upon him were to add to the terrors of dissolution; far less disquieting were the cold and pallid walls, the vacant air, the droning silence.

'Let me be,' he whispered; 'I shall die gently.'

Some one late that night, stumbling to a neighbouring garret by the gusty flare of a candle, paused outside the sick-room. The door crept open in a gap, and Dick saw the face of the little serving maid, unkempt and flurried, framed distressfully in the long aperture. His eyes and his lean finger invited her towards the chair. Staring with inflated eyes, she obeyed the gesture, and sat, her candle on her knee, her mouth agape in a pant of wondering fear. Dick dumbly watched the ill-shapen features. This then was the last human figure of which he might have sense. Other phantoms might rise in his mind and mingle there in a shadowy morrice, but this alone would move and feel and speak with continuity and independence. Them he could exclude from his weary brain in a twinkling, at the call of a fly buzzing on the pane; while this alone should stay there persistent, should dance to no

invisible strings, should stir with young vigour,
should be fulfilled of lively motions. He could
not predict her actions; she would be gay with
surprises. She would answer his mute eyes by
some correspondent expression of her features,
would interpret his impalpable thoughts into the
flesh of performance, would watch him with some
sorrow, would, perchance, tend him with some
pity and lament him with some sincerity. She
was too young to have this doctor's neglect of
death ; and with this poor creature's solemn awe
and childish sympathy he might pass from the
presence of a warm and living soul, not wholly
discarded of a world of which he still was part.

She had recovered from her emotions, and sat
staring about the room with a chastened wonder.
It was all too familiar to her ; and yet, it seemed,
the discoloured walls, the sooty roof, the cracked
chair, were all invested with new aspects. Her
gaze returned to him. Her face was small and
pitiful ; her years were few weighed against her
labours. Dick strove at a smile ; he fixed his
spectral eyes upon her. His wits were shining
clear and luminous, but he was past speech or
action. In his mouth the thought he would have
put into words rattled at its prison-bars. At the
sound the girl started. It was as if the sudden
irruption upon the quiet had frightened her.
She gave a tiny cry, which was suddenly hushed
in her throat as though she had remembered the

sick-chamber. A panic sprang out in her face. She rose, and, watching him fearfully, backed quickly and noiselessly from the room, leaving the still figure with its eyes riveted upon the door.

WAS ever woman in so distressful a case?' she cried, flinging her hands with a smack upon the water.

I rapped my boot in meditation. 'The devil's in the job,' said I; 'I can see no way out of the predicament. It is certain, then,' I asked, 'that these garments went afloat?'

'Certain!' she echoed. 'No sooner was I sporting in the shallows than this libertine of a river had snatched them in a twinkling; and away they scurried, shooting on the current like a racer. Certain!' she wailed. 'Faith, I chased them down the stream to the brink of exhaustion.'

'I have gone up and down the banks,' said I, 'and there's never a visible vestige.' She lifted a white arm out of the pool and threw back her streaming hair.

'You have been very good,' said she. 'Some kindly providence surely despatched you on this walk.'

''Twas a vague humour,' I explained, 'an in-

different desire of solitude. I had been used so
ill at the manor that the sight of my fellows
grew distasteful, and ——'

'It is no time for reproaches,' she broke in
quickly; 'you had nothing beyond your deserts, I
vow.' I shrugged my shoulders. 'The question
is,' said she, 'this inglorious position of mine. I
pray you, put your wits to work. Oh, that this
caprice ever took my silly fancy!'

The river ran in little whirls and singing eddies
between its heavy banks; deep buried in the
quiet pool she clung distressfully to the osiers of
the tiny islet; overhead shone the noontide sun
from the depths of a blue heaven; and in the
pleasant shadows of the willows I sat and looked
at her. 'Let us consider the facts with care,'
said I. '*Imprimis:* the village lies five miles in
the valley. Should I start forthwith, 'twill be
nigh two hours ere you shall once more have the
liberty of clothes.'

'Two hours in this ticklesome stream!' she
cried; 'two hours of chance perils!'

'*Item,*' said I, 'of chance hopes also. May be
at a cottage ——'

'None within miles,' she wailed. ''Tis a
wilderness, a wilderness. Else I had not ventured
on this prank.'

'H'm,' said I. '*Item:* your sex, ere this, has
masqueraded in knee-breeches. As for myself,
even though 'twas not you in the case, two hours

in these cool waters were no great penance this midsummer. Such as it be, this poor raiment is at your service.'

'Twould fit me so ill!' she complained; 'and to be seen so I should die of shame.' Her own whims had reduced us to a quandary, and I stared at a loss for a single suggestion more. Silence fell upon us. Through the ruffled mirror of the pool the contour of her white body wavered and zigzagged. The sun glistered on her golden tresses through the osier branches. A sense of her beauty took me at this absurd time very pleasantly, and I laughed softly at the fancy.

'Those golden locks—' said I; 'what better vesture for you than that glorious hair?'

A pink flush got up in her cheeks; she turned away her head.

'You are unkind,' said she, 'and the jest is in poor taste.'

''Twas no jest, indeed,' I protested warmly.

'Then,' said she plumply, 'you have taken leave of your wits.'

'Maybe,' I answered. 'They have bid me good-bye these many weeks I have known you; and to have come suddenly upon you thus has robbed me of my remaining judgment. I had dreamed of river-nymphs in such a place. On my soul, you play the Naiad most delicately well.'

She smiled faintly at my speech, but in a moment a shadow leapt over her face.

'Oh, it is absurd!' she cried. 'This odious country! and this is all come of my affectation of the rustic habit! London at her dullest held at least no such embarrassment. Oh! 'tis humiliating. I hate you. Go.'

'I cannot but think,' said I gravely, 'that this adventure is in the nature of a retribution. Yet, for all you have entreated me so evilly for weeks together, my gay coquette, I cannot,' quoth I, 'endure to triumph over you.'

With that I turned to be gone, but ere I had taken a dozen paces a noise in the copse arrested my attention; and next moment a rustic maiden pushed through the underwood and stepped out upon the open patch by the river. She wore a dainty gown that swayed about her ankles as she walked, and her high bodice paused over her bosom for all the world as though she were a shepherdess from Arcady. Her blue eyes stared widely from myself to the water and its pretty nymph.

'Ho! ho!' said I. 'Good-day to you, young mistress of the roses. You have come in the nick of time to wrest a creature from despair.' I ducked to her and pointed to the osiers.

'For shame!' says she, eyeing me with some scorn.

'Indeed,' said I. 'There's nothing against

I

me. She needs your help, good soul. For by some gross misfortune her pretty robes are all gone a-swimming for the sea; and she is left shivering in the current, with none but me to give her pity.'

'You were better away, sir,' says my Audrey.

'You speak truth,' I answered. 'And I will leave her now in your hands. You shall dress and compose her anew; so shall the mishap be but an adventure to be remembered with laughter.'

She turned a pitying glance upon my lady.

'But, sir,' said she, 'from this 'tis a good hour to my home, and this dimity is all I have. What I stand in, that is mine; and no more.'

I made a gesture of despair. 'Come,' said I, 'let us at least discuss the occasion plainly,' and I drew her to the margin of the stream, where my poor naiad waited expectantly.

'She will procure something?' she burst out.

'Alas, madam,' I answered, 'she has but her own upon her.'

'I shall die of cold—and of shame,' she murmured; 'pray you, be generous,' she begged, 'lend me those garments of yours, and you shall have them back with interest. As one woman may beg of another, so I entreat you.' My Audrey shook her head; she eyed her lady-sister pitifully; glanced at her own pretty gown and then at me; flushed red to her eyebrows and

shook her head again. In the embarrassment of
the ensuing silence I turned away.

' You shall settle it between you. I'm for the
village with all speed,' quoth I hastily, and would
have made off.

' No, no,' called her voice from the osiers.
' You would not abandon me so. This wretch
will do nothing in my behalf. Think of the perils
between now and your rescue. I beseech you, stay.'

In her solicitude she raised herself a little by
the osiers, and lifted a pleading face to me ; the
water washed and rippled over her bosom. So
distraught and sorrowful were those eyes, that
meeting them I had not the heart to desert her,
but took a sudden resolution to hazard all for
her release.

' By heaven !' I exclaimed, ' you shall have
those garments, or I die.'

She thanked me with her eyes. I turned to
Audrey, standing with wonder in the shade of the
copse. ' My dear,' said I, ' this is the very devil.
I pray you will reconsider your decision. For
look you, here is the case. You were plainly
come for a dip ; let us employ this dimity of yours
during your performance in the river. Come.'

Something in my manner may have alarmed
her ; it was as though she feared I would strip
her perforce of her property ; and she retired into
the seclusion of the copse, peeping over a bush
at me.

'Look you,' said I, 'let me speak plainly. I
throw myself upon your mercy. For the better
part of this day has she borne with this sorry
plight; her eyes are wet with tears, not water;
she hath wrung her hands until they weary; her
heart is aching with despair and shame. I entreat
you to show some pity. In a privy coign of this
dingle you might ensure yourself against all
observation, basking in the comfortable sun.
Then in a little you shall be bedecked in the
gayest of raiment, and a carriage, to boot, shall
take you to your home. Oh, she is the most
generous, and her favours are the rarest.'

My Audrey slowly dropped behind the bush.
'And think again,' quoth I, fearful she was to
fly off in her alarm; 'she has shivered in this
cool stream for hours, and has gotten a cold to
perish from. So fair a lady and so vile a death!
Shall it comfort you, my little tender-heart, to
reflect one day that but for this cold prudery
she who now sleeps i' the grave might still be
dancing in her royal beauty? Her fate lies in
your hands. Be pitiful and she will live; refuse
her and she must die.'

I caught a whimper from behind the bush, and
as I paused, a hand stole out, reluctant, with a
gown. I laid it by me.

'And what,' I asked, 'must be my future if this
tragic fate befall?' 'Alas!' I cried to Heaven,
'the world must be a wilderness for me hence-

forth. For she and I were wed but three months
since, and all these days shall I have striven to
shield her from harm—in vain ; and to think
now, that this miserable weakling of a river that
might not drown a cat must tear my beloved
from me for the sake of one pretty prude !'

'You are married?' she whispered from the
bush.

'Is it not so ?' I called to the islet.

'Indeed, indeed !' she answered.

She thrust me forth her petticoat.

'But there is worse,' said I. 'Madam, my wife
is in the most delicate health. This assuredly
were not for mention save to your friendly ears,
but hark you ——' and I whispered into the bush.

'Is it so ?' she asked, weeping.

'Is it not the truth?' I asked across the
water.

'I'll swear to it,' says my naiad.

She thrust me forth her smock.

'My dear,' I said, 'those dainty shoes and
elegant hosen ; and we will leave you under the
heaviest of obligations.'

She put them forth with a pretty dimpled arm,
and I rose to my feet with my spoils, triumphant.

'And now, my tender Audrey,' I continued, 'I
wish you joy of the sunshine and your rest. A
bed of soft leaves and cool fern will suffice for
slumber, and if you be tempted there is the water
purling at your feet. Anon you shall dress and

drive with the most ravishing lady at His Majesty's Court.'

I ran down to the water's edge, and exhibited my burden to my lady's sparkling eyes.

'I vow,' she said, 'you are the best of men. I am sorry I have used you badly. Begone, begone, sir,' she cried, laughing. 'I will give you thanks and to spare hereafter.'

'Softly,' I murmured, 'softly, my naiad. I have bought this wardrobe at a heavy price of lies; my conscience quails and shrivels at the recollection. And what has cost me so dear—my soul's salvation, must surely go to the sale for its worth.'

She regarded me doubtfully, fearfully.

'What would you have?' she asked.

I dangled the smock before her. 'This,' I said, 'should fetch a precious price, no doubt, but I am content to dispose most cheaply of my wares. We shall walk home together to the manor.'

'Agreed,' says she, smiling.

I took another garment from the heap.

'By all tradition in the knowledge of men,' I resumed, 'this hath a value beyond estimate. 'Tis indispensable. But I am in a melting mood. You shall take my arm and use me most sweetly?'

'If it must be so,' said she.

'And this,' I said, 'I must suppose you would not be without. Well, you shall redeem it likewise. A price, a price, not overhigh in respect of your needs, but high enough I grant you. For

the intrinsic value of this thing I care not a jot;
I am to reckon from your penury. It is yours,
but you shall give me what I have begged in vain
these many days—you shall permit me to salute
you.'

'Sir,' said she angrily, 'you have put all your
virtues to the hammer. But if you demand it
and will act thus scurvily by my troubles, in
God's name have your way and be done.'

I laughed and left her; and in the briefest
space we were on the road for the manor. But
now, although she took my arm and walked beside
me she was openly traversing the second article
of our bargain; for she maintained a sullen
silence all the way, or at the most replied to me
in monosyllables. This breach was beyond my
toleration, and though I did not rally her upon
it by the way, her conduct weighed upon me all
that afternoon. It seemed that we had fallen
further apart than ever, and at last I sought her
later in the day and reproached her faithless-
ness.

'I have kept the letter,' she retorted. 'I have
none but literal obligations to one who would
presume on my misery.'

'It was a scurvy trick,' said I cheerfully; 'but
I have not yet taken advantage of your consent.
Indeed, there was no word of time in our conditions, you will perceive.' She looked up at
me.

'You will not exact it?' she asked quickly.

'I said not so,' I answered. 'Let us come to a conclusion. Will you marry me?'

I confronted her seriously. She laughed.

'Marry you!' she said, and laughed again.

'And why not?' I asked, 'I have long been at your feet. Come, dear, will you love me?' She put back her head and laughed in her chair. 'If you knew,' I said roughly, 'how much you have sworn to this day, you would scarce laugh so heartily.'

'Sworn to?' she said, stopping suddenly, 'what do you mean? Have you said ——'

'Well,' I explained, 'I had the purchase of your garments, you will recall.'

'Those lies—what were they?' she cried, a flash of colour in her cheeks.

'We were man and wife,' I replied, 'and ——'

'Well?' she urged.

I wavered, and my eyes sought the ground.

The red burned in her face; she made as though she would cry out with passion; but meeting my beseeching gaze her eyes fell, and she was mute.

'Come,' I said hotly, 'I will only exact that article upon your consent to this petition. See, I tear the contract into pieces. Now, sweet, be my wife,' and I put out my hand.

She gave me hers, half smiling, half frowning, and the third clause was fulfilled on the instant.

Suddenly I started back. 'Good Lord,' I exclaimed, 'I had forgot poor Audrey!'

She stared for a moment, and then burst into laughter.

ER complexion is so exquisitely fair that there is no comparison for it; to look for one would be to dishonour her loveliness. It is strange that though she is so dear to me I cannot describe her with precision. I am conscious that she is fairer than I know, for my sight dims a little in regarding her; her beauty is blurred for me in its own irradiance. As I near her eyes, which are the full centre of her glory, a haze sets in, bedewing her mistily. I am content to know her thus, though I should wrong her great perfection. I would not have you think her pale or waxen; for those eyes and her canopy of hair are full of colour, and her cheeks are softly tinted. I cannot give you any image of her for the infirmity of words. I have put about to describe her, but there are no terms for her; her loveliness is new to the world with herself. Her face is so delicately beautiful that I cannot separate its characters; in itself it is an ultimate thought. Yet from each one of her features I should know

her face, they are so rare to me. When I look
at her I am conscious mainly of her eyes, though
should I meet them not the rest fills me so
divinely that when at last she glances to me my
delight flows over in esteem. Observing the
conduct of others, I wonder sometimes if aught is
wrong with my vision that I see her so lustrous
when they can be placid. I know not why she
should be different from her fellows. Of her
dress I can tell but little, for its contemplation
would lead me from her face. Yet they say, it
meetly clothes a gracious body. If it is meet for
hers, there is no higher praise for it.

I would not you held mine to be a common
affection ; yet I am at a loss in bare words to
prove it above the general enchantment. If you
could see her, it would be the argument. Her
favour has ordered my life so wonderfully as to
make me a stranger to myself. I have desires
and feelings greater than you would attribute to
to our mortal clay ; and I am constrained to put
my delicate sensations into poor thoughts, and
these into poorer language. I have grown subtler
since I met her. I have not yet resolved the
secret of my fascination ; she makes of my heart
and mind a dim confusion. When she speaks I
marvel to find her material ; her voice distresses
me with its reminder that there are times when
others listen to it and not I. I do not know
whether it is this or the turn of her head moves

me most; I thrill at both; but when her eyes
touch me she has no other magic. I discern her
smile afar, and then I rejoice with her. Her
happiness has illumined the whole street for me
ere she has turned the corner. In my thought I
watch her by the hours in her daily progress,
hanging upon her changes with tremulous delight, till I have forgot her bodily absence. I
have striven at times to conceive a being of a
finer mould, but my imagination has foundered in
the venture. The most ingenious of my supposi-
tions was pitiful beside her. I would keep all
harm from her, though, as she holds me, so surely
must she hold all else within her orders. My
reverence would protect her even from myself.
When her skirts have swept by me I have been
minded to take them to me, but have shrunk back
lest the perfidy of my kiss should taint her. I
fear to pluck my rose out of the morning lest perchance it bloom sweeter on the stem. And yet I
would have her always by me; the departing
rustle of her gown is a dirge for me. I bear about
with me the marks of my passion, so that to my
friends I am become as a fool. I am grown so
inseparable from her in my thoughts that I
am become her shadow; to recall her image is to
see my own stark face. I am fallen into a by-
word to myself because of her: she stands between
me and the immediate concerns of life. Time
has laid me under heavy bonds, who was from the

first a captive. I have no thought or feeling
through the day that does not turn to her. Her
soul stands now for mine; there is but one
between us, and that is hers. At nights I summon her picture to me ere I fall asleep; her
vision drifts before me till morning. In the dawn
I take her from my heart, and regard her linea-
ments with dispassionate remoteness. I call her
then my dream and my illusion, and vow to live
more sanely, as one who knows the gross roots of
human affection. But this thought of treason
passes in the second, and I fall to crying that the
world is mad, not I. I have sworn that the
secrets of the earth are ignoble, but at her smile
I have forsworn myself. It is odd so exquisite a
sentiment as mine should be of human derivation.
I am aware that you will hold my rapture to be
compound of final instincts, clear, catholic,
unmarvellous. But there are deep mysteries in
this tangle of Nature. I will deny all earthliness
in her. There is naught but Heaven anigh the
transfigured soul. I am grown loftier now. I am
grown graver too. I have become the prey of fell
terrors. Each day an added impulse makes my
life more ethereal; each day my eyes are more
familiar with her beauty, my lips with her name.
But each day, too, I have the burden of a new
fear, that she must meet the chances of the world.
I dread the night for its dark vicissitudes; I have
a horror of the uncertainties of day. There is a

word I dare not whisper to myself; it is a spectre stalking through my heart. There are such fears abroad in my life that I am a quaking coward. I ponder daily upon mortality. Will not God who has given such goodliness preserve it? I set out with a vain glory that I had found this pearl; I am now the humblest of His creatures supplicating mercy.

THE MERRY COMPANY

W E are met with a merry company at our elbows, and are bent upon putting Sorrow to shame. In this room shall be none but the gay and the glorious; God send the others to the pit! Thought pulls at his brows, Care weeps like a jade: let the unhandsome couple go match out of doors, out of sight, out of hearing. There is no favour we would require of Fortune but to commend us to the jocund, to withhold us from the sad. This sober melancholy is no divine contrivance but a manufacture of the Devil, wherewith he would have us mock our human composition. We make no terms with Sorrow at our board; he turns in a rout at our menace, and we fall to scoffing at his flight. Time has not seen this craven in our midst since man issued his primeval challenge. Whatever changes pass before us we have ever the trick of laughter. Without, though the street roar with noises or be silent with dread, silence nor uproar may trouble us here: our merriment is secure, our joy is

immutable, we measure out delights with the
measure of our lives. There be none here but
have grinned through the feast since Time first
set them at the board; grief is a breath that fleets
ere the features take note of it, a cough, an itch,
a blink that hath no place in time. Despair
has no home here; from the roar and flyting of
this revelry trouble slinks away. To assume a
melancholy visage were the surest discomfiture,
for our clean wits fall upon it, white-hot, ere the
expression be set; and the heavy lines turn for
sheer shame into a gamesome smile. Nay, there
is none here but the roysterer, the free of heart,
the quick of head, the heedless, the all-merry. To
be wise, we say, is to be the fool of circumstance;
let the mind run only upon the latest chuckle of
your neighbour. A dull dog, we say, is a rebuke
unto his Maker. He hath bequeathed you a
monstrously well-meaning gift, sirs; pray guard
Him from the knowledge of His failures. Is
there an error in the type? As you are gentle-
men, pardon this faulty architecture. Two dis-
positions has He given you: the one unto mirth,
the other unto morals. Are you mad that you
halt between them? Life is to us all here a
swift pageant of delights; one ensueth upon the
other, grin upon grin, jape upon jape, laughter
upon laughter, content upon contentment, continuously rounding infinitely to the end. Yet
our feast hath no end, as it hath no beginning;

for they that were are no longer; and when we
shall be not, others shall have our places. Against
this solid defiance Death is but a poor antagonist,
this vain browbeater, this uncomely visitant. He
hath grown mad at his figures, and hath the
thought, poor zany, to lap up the eternal.

Upon us now and then in our rudest tempers
breaks this Apparition. We hear the still small
knock, and lo! the familiar spectre at the door,
glancing with infinite quiet about the company.
But he hath no terrors for us; for our goodly
fellowship is immortal, and his presence is stale
and intimate. He has endured upon us thus,
this weak wreck of a mighty spirit, from the
back of old Time; he has become a convivial
fellow to us, so often do we see him in our cups.
A veteran mild-mannered acquaintance, he can
work no harm upon us, for he taketh one by one,
and as each goes another enters; the place
empties not: it fills and refills; more cry for
entrance at the windows. He hath no impression
upon us; his jaws drop at our numbers; he
winces from our vivacity; he has set himself the
maddest task. Yea, and we use him despitefully.
If he enter, he too must be gay; we will have
none in our presence but is a jester. He is our
familiar, our seneschal, our janitor, our meagre-
visaged keeper, the associate of hoary age. He
must come in to us with smiles for us, or we flout
him. 'To your work,' we say, 'old Satan!'

This Death has come to wear a face of the most grotesque importance; he has taken his office seriously and with pride, and is grown most deadly solemn. He raps with hesitation, and stalks in with a religious air, forsooth, as on a mission from the preachers. 'Come in,' we shout, 'come in and take your choice of us. Have no fears, old wry-face; here is no squeamish but an impudent company.' And when his business is done we put him to the door. We have no patience with this grey and serious spectre, with his grin sedate, with his mien austere, with his gait sanctimonious and exemplary. 'Out with him,' we cry, 'if he will not gibe;' and with one for his fellow he issues forth, a blank and moody ghost. 'Is that old vulture-face gone out?' we call; 'here's to his body disparate from his soul!' The dropping goblets clank; the table roars. The hours slip by, slip by; we shall have him again shortly if we pause. Swift flies the newest humour round and round; the hot blood clamours in the veins; the spirit mounting from the fiery heart breaks out upon the tongue; the rafters echo—we are met at a feast, and old Death himself may not stay us. One leans to another and whispers; the jest flits lightly; Disdain is our only mother. There is no moment of awe at our board; there is never a hush, never an hour but has wings. Is any mute? Let Death take him for the next; he knows not the way of life. Quit,

quit, an you have not the fashion of merriment;
ancient, staid, respectable Death were your fitter
companion. Hark! there is the uncertain step
once more; and there is the hesitant knock.
'Enter! enter!' we cry; and lo, the grisly
creature in our midst again, spelling upon his
lean fingers, with his silent eyes. Nodding, drinking, laughing, winking—out we go.

HEAR, all ye that make beauty your god, and be warned of me in respect of this woman. Let him that is without her range, and him that moveth in her circle, consider my words which are of wisdom.

She has the witchery of the Devil, yet is she nearer in her soul to Heaven than all they that do no evil in your midst. From the outset of your acquaintance she will be to you as the most wholly adorable of all idols, whose beauty is a mockery unto the Decalogue. She will smile with such eyes as shall go shining through your solitary soul, making manifest to you its great emptiness. She will bend to you with so lithe a grace that you will have no space in your thoughts but for the immediate sensation; it will set you aflame on the instant. There is ineffable abandonment in her movements that was learnt of houris or of faëry. Her lips are the gates of Paradise. I am aware how fatuous is this summary of her charm, and yet merely to class her as lovely were to shrink from one's

148

duty of homage. If you will suppose these and far subtler graces compact in one favoured body, you will perchance conceive with what show of resistance you will be like to approach her. Assuredly you will regard your finest efforts as unworthy tributes in her service, and account yourself blessed to be admitted to this new religion. For the neophytes in her worship she has a particular kindness, and will thus display to you such natural sympathies as will reveal her the most tender of her tender sex. Indeed, there is nothing too mean for her pity nor too remote for her kind thought. You yourself will consider that you are followed day-long by her gracious regard, and that in the night your memory is contemplated by those frank and faithful eyes. Her heart, you will vow, corroborates her face, and there is none since God made Eve, such an epitome of excellence.

But I that alone among worshippers have the gift of clear discernment cry you a warning in the streets. You have the folly in your blood and the blink of the sun in your eyes. Pause ere you venture nearer this divinity that to me as to you is the centre-piece of earth; that has put me to despair above all, the greatest of her sufferers by reason of his most arrogant desire. What she shines in your eyes, that is she truly—sweet-hearted, gracious, beautiful, and free; but she has put a bar 'twixt herself and the supreme

passion. Hence shall you behold her as she is.
That smile of hers, in truth the significant index
of a kindly heart, and those admirable affections, ·
its necessary expression, are of such a ruthless
sanity that it is not possible to be fully just to
them upon a longer acquaintance. They appear
a mockery which are but her inborn grace. For
she herself is without guile or evil purpose, un-
touched of *diablerie*, open-souled, gay, light of
heart, serene, indifferent, the most natural, self-
revealed, unhesitating idol of this world. Out of
her glass her fair face must surely start each
morning an immortal surprise upon its owner;
yet I will swear it is odds she has forgotten it
when she meets you. It is true, the admiration
in your gaze will prick her memory; but the
vanity is passing, the picture of her own perfection flits like a shadow over the sunlight, too
brief for recognition, too familiar for regard.
The simplicity of her unconsciousness is inordinate. Each day she goes into the whirl of the
world with a dainty delight; each night she whips
out of it with a wreathed smile, half for these
dear done pleasures, half for the happy morrow.
Become by her pretty gestures, she has fallen
into them through no desire of attraction, but
fortuitously as to the habit born, from the very
persuasion of her own individuality. Yet she is
aware they are engaging, as she has knowledge of
her own loveliness, and with the most surprising

candour will discuss them with you, should she
have the whim. The whim is her master; she is
at the mercy of the moment's inspiration. It
will bid her confess you all things; there shall be
no secrets between you and herself; before you
the inner mysteries of beauty will be laid bare
with convincing sincerity. The idle humour is
like blood in her veins, the active spirit of her
being. Nothing is set for you, nothing prepared.
If you shall behold her at one particular moment
transcendent above her lovely self, it is not of
her arrangement; she lays no mine against your
heart's integrity. It is true she has the eyes of a
woman, and discerns your affection ere it come to
your own knowledge. But the discovery has small
interest for her, for she has long known that you
too must join the worshippers; and what matters
one in a crowd! If it were not you, lo! it must
be another; and, to do her justice, she would as
lief be kind to you as to him. Even were it in
her power, she would never prohibit you from
your folly. Though the cruelty of her beauty is
so notorious to herself, she doubtless takes a
certain pleasure in its handiwork; if so be, that
is, no incompatible caprice be dancing in her
veins. She will never, be assured, withhold her
eyes for fear of their danger. The rest is 'twixt
yourself and your Maker. Save on the sway of
the moment, her regard for one is no greater
than for another. She will deal with you as with

me, with me as with another, and will think it a
pity that some should bear their fate so ill.
It was no fault in her; Fate must be to blame,
and neither she nor you. There have been few
occasions, I should judge, when she has been out
of temper with the importunity of her admirers;
out of her excellent pity and kindness she will
not suffer it to interfere with her fastidious
friendliness. Though by this her satisfaction
must be of the smallest, she will hear your
passion with the utmost indulgence. Nay, her
excellence is so preposterous that when you are
describing your rare feelings she will positively
simulate an air of sympathetic interest, as though
you were telling of your influenza; and in the
end will condole with you and wonder aloud what
cure will meet your case. When you arrive her
pleasure is free and facile; when you leave, she
is unfeignedly regretful. Throughout you are
part of her necessary environment in a most
delightful life; and the law of her nature is to
be tolerant and kind. Thus, should you come
into her acquaintance, you will find her: your
ecstasy and your despair, as she is mine, who am
the foremost and most forlorn of all her victims.

THE DEAD IMMORTALS

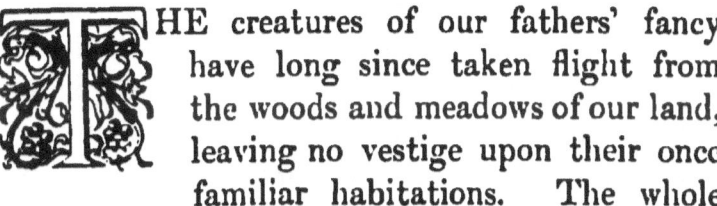

HE creatures of our fathers' fancy have long since taken flight from the woods and meadows of our land, leaving no vestige upon their once familiar habitations. The whole length of this island, heretofore populous with dainty presences, lies now forlorn and empty in the possession of inferior hands. The soil is turned to ignoble uses, broken with the plough and the harrow, and the hills that once tinkled to the laughter of the fairy now smoke from a hundred brazen mouths; or at best stand silent in a melancholy reticence. Each hour brings its own disillusionment, but it seems a pity we have lost our hold upon this pretty faith, which ran against no whim of modern progress. The red sun takes the humours from the grass, and the wind set the trees a-quiver, but they warm not, neither fan, the elfin folk in the quiet glades. All these are fled, rapt into a limbo of forgotten myths, where gnomes and djinns and trolls keep them spectral company. The lively imagination

153

of the human kind has fashioned a creditable variety of these creatures, and now that the art is gone with the capacity of belief, we cold inheritors of the ages may take our choice from a motley society of perished immortals. For myself, I have little liking for the Oriental invention; one could not have used these lank black monsters with special tenderness or confidence. They were too oppressive in their distance from humanity, and it had been impossible to invest them with the common graces of intercourse. They were not constructed for company, and at most might be tamed into some sort of grudging slavery by mystic rings and signals. For the more part their work was evil like their persons, and you could not but feel that they were happiest torturing some individual enemy out of his wits. They were potent enough, it is true, and had an admirable gift of incorporeality which must have served their masters at odd times; but their grotesque and ingenious personalities put them out of human sympathy. One could never have been quite secure with them; while they lasted, society must have ever been within a pinch of chaos. The djinns would have made a black and a bitter business of the world.

The Greeks, on the other hand, showed a far more fastidious taste in conjecture. Knowing of nothing more delightful than themselves, they proceeded to build up a heaven upon this basis, withdrawing therefrom the least idyllic elements of their own nature. My sentiment has always lain at the mercy of their mythology, but yet I cannot in my mind wholly acquit the plan of imperfection. The gods and the goddesses, with the various nymphs and resident deities of earth, though a charming society, cunningly and elegantly devised, come too near our human selves to keep their necessary dignity. The notion that the divine and beautiful beings should make a playground of our favoured planet is of itself ravishing beyond question; but still I have that critical objection in my eye. They were too little remote, too omnipresent, too casual and inevitable in their dealings; they could have been no surprise to one of any decent experience in the world, and must have worn themselves indeed into a commonplace. This would have been of little consequence had they been intrinsically superior to or more profound than their subjects; but they were insufficiently commanding to enforce respect, and thus, no doubt, they came to pass current lightly, at times even for a joke. And yet life was after all the fuller for the fine superstition. It was not indigenous here nor even naturalised, but it is pleasant to reflect that, had Pan not died, he and his train might have visited England. Nowhere would he have found a more free and fitting paradise. I can with difficulty refer the system to our own woods and streams, so long the haunts of other creatures, yet the white flash of naiad limbs in the running water would add some glory to a landscape. These nymphs were but feminine, if of a little finer clay; they had the form and faculty of woman, no more; but their tastes were entirely original, and though they shared with their mortal sisters the sexual frailty, and were nothing moved thereby, yet they employed a delicate art in the occasions of their appearance, and the vision of them leaned unto the romantical. You might indeed have surprised them skimming and gliding through the translucent shallows, and taken them at first sight for a bevy of girls at play, but your visit would have a mightier consequence than merely to start the pack blushing and squealing. You have no opportunity of this experience now; not even in Greece. The river goes purling and loitering on his way, for all the world as though never a naiad had dipped from his banks. There is a certain desolation in the thought. Poppies and willows and marigolds and marguerites you shall find, but never a shining body with tossing hair afloat from shallow to shallow, through deep upon deep. The pools are ruffled only by the trout and the grayling or the flitting gnats; the spirits are clean gone from their accustomed places.

It was a pretty humour to people the woods also with these rare inhabitants, but there was little proportion in the thought. For the fair

and sprightly hamadryads were really better
suited to the smiling meadows than to the grim
forests. By the side of knotted boles and gnarled
branches the lithe and lovely limbs would make
an uncouth contrast, incongruous to the reason,
however enlivening to wayfarers conscious of the
peeping eyes. In this respect our Northern fancy
has observed a severe propriety, as indeed throughout its inventions it has been most sensitive and
exact. For the forests there were gnomes,
goblins for the dark places of the hills, elves and
fairies for the meadowlands and dales : mermaids
also to wash about the seas. The rivers managed
somehow to slip out of this scheme, though doubtless a fluent occasion of elfin happiness. How
peculiarly appropriate was this division of power !
It was the pretty issue of a dream more spiritual
than the Greek's, more familiar than the
Oriental's. The countryside was crowded with
these presences dancing somewhere betwixt invisi-
bility and materiality, hovering like things
unshapen in the eyesight. Should you close your
lids at moonlight, they would flicker before you
between sleeping and waking, with the transi-
ent reality of darting flames ; in and out, in and
out of the vision they would fly, till, grown auda-
cious from the indolence of your recognition,
they would descend into the warm life, and come
skipping breast-high amid the daisies. The grin
with which those elves would approach you was

of the merriest and most affable, and their antics
were vastly entertaining.   Not Puck nor Cobweb
nor any of them, you could swear, would do you
harm.   They must have their own small chuckle,
being of a humorous turn; but the jest against
you was ever to be amiable.   And their fairy
companions were models of elegance in miniature;
the daintiest fry that ever presumed on immortality, large-eyed and wonder-mouthed, fragile
and delicate beyond apprehension.   Could you
steal through the woods to the verge of the open
glade you might behold them upon any clear
night, a merry band, fluttering in a ring about
the ancient groaning oaks, kicking their elfin
heels, tumbling and rioting through the long
grass-stalks, a pretty company of dishevelled
spirits gone mad at the fulness of the moon.
They were unlike the gloomy djinns or the very
human naiads : theirs was the very spirit of fantastic delight, the pure ecstasy of disembodiment.
No less than the sad-eyed mermaid became her
melancholy sea did those gay mannikins and fays
fulfil the humour of the cheerful countryside.   It
is in all ways a pitiful reflection that they are
gone.   But just as a noise from your hiding-place
within the copse must have sent them all into an
instant dissolution, so too at some big roar in the
world's progress have they vanished o' nights for
ever, and only silence now holds the long valleys.

TO ANY GREYBEARD

YOU are now distant many winters from your prime, yet you were once as I am; and I entreat you, pardon me if, foreboding my own declension, I reflect upon your state. How long you have lived! What a term of years has fallen to you, if you will but consider! There are threescore and more of venerable annals in your memory, and to live a twelvemonth is to see strange things. You are yourself a fraction of the world's age, and must embrace some mighty circumstances in her history. You are no cipher, therefore; for, even though it were against your will, you have been a constituent of change in a planet which is part of the universe. No wonder this knowledge disposes you to disdain the uninfluential young, for your movements have helped to set the stars a-tingle. You are of my forerunners and my founders; I am of your manufacture, unawares; were it not for your white locks I should have no being. I bow to you: for you

I have a reverent gratitude. Shall I be like you
sometime ? Let me look upon my fate.

These long grey years have taught you many
things, for Time's is the only school. When I
consider with what a fantastic armoury you set
forth, I find it marvellous that you have got so
far in safety; though it is long since you cast
away your last ineptitude, I wonder you did not
perish in those early days. But now you are
equipped after Time's own heart, and nothing
but misadventure of the flesh can make a dint
upon you. What great lessons he has impressed
on you since first you came under his stick ! You
have learned to regret not nor to mourn, not to
refuse nor to deny, to be silent, to sit at ease, to
laugh. In your perilous passage to so remote a
rock as now you occupy, you have gathered a
cheerful stock of wit, pilfering from a thousand
forgotten sources ; and with this your grey
thoughts keep most incongruous company. How
is it such a fellowship does not appear unto you
bitter ? I fancy you must have lost your sense
of the grotesque. Your continued joyous existence is most unnatural, for you have violated
every spontaneous injunction of your youth.
There was never an instinctive longing in you
that Experience did not crush ; yet so has she
shaped you to a grinning disregard that you
stand exquisitely adjusted to her. When you
were as I am now, you turned from those who

were as now you are, with a restrained contempt,
a noticeable pity, an incipient fear. It did not
seem to you that they were well, alive. You had
looked for their disappearance at fifty, but they
surprised you. So do you us, your grandsons. Is
it not plain to you that in your youth you pursued objects which were shadows? And, were they
substantial, you are a score of years beyond them
now. What keeps you alive? What can you
have left for your ruin of a human frame, for
your pillaged temple of a body?

Yet you take life with the ease and indifference
of twenty, with no greater anxiety than has the
youth on whom a golden world is dawning. It
is true his model is not yours to the finger-tips,
for you have the secret of living with ease only
and not with elegance. Yet you are more fortunate than he; for though like you he lives in the
ever-flowing present, there comes a time when he
fears the future, while for you there is only the
past. Between you and him lie all the terrors,
the sorrows, the failures, the tragedies of life.
He is not yet upon the tide; you have been
washed to the beyond. All great desires have
left you; the passions that are born of Life, yet
wear their mother to the grave, have fled from a
house which holds now but the desire of existence,
the passion of self-preservation. You keep yourself in an even balance with external accidents so
that they do not disarrange your equable mood,

and time has formed this habit so perfectly that
you yield only to some material disappointment
of a primary order. Threescore years have turned ·
you out a most dainty *connoisseur* of the daily
round, and it is only outrage of this taste smacks
to you of misfortune.   If your dinner misfits, 'tis
an offence for the stocks ; but happily you will
forget it with the day, as you forget all things.
And yet in a way you have but now begun
to remember.   The champions of old time lie
buried in your youth, and their memories are
your monopoly.   Jealousy died when you resigned
the passions, so your delight is at its highest in
the company of those who can remember with
you.   But the memories of coëvals are rarely at
one, and each will add a new note of admiration,
each will extend into the most astonishing par-
entheses.   These asides are better than your main
theses, being instantaneous miniatures of your
life, whereas the latter are apt to be cut to one
length, excerpts from larger reminiscences, filch-
ings from the public knowledge.   But this hark-
back is your sweetest diversion, and I often
wonder how you bear the passage of your com-
peers.   For as your grey beard turns white, one
by one they go by you into the darkness.   How
long have they been falling away who could
remember with you once the great occasion of
your manhood ? Once you could crack with
many, but now your recollections overlap with

few. You have not even a fellow to recall the
dish old Terrè served upon that summer night
sixty years since. For the lack of a stimulus you
too are forgetting, and if your friends give you
leave Terrè will soon pass from you as all else is
passing; even the fragrance of a dish must leave
you at last. One would think that this growing
isolation would strike a chill into your bones;
but though I watch I do not observe you to
tremble. I could vow there is not one of you
looks across the border enviously; not one blinks
at the open prospect. You have no grudge
against your position, nor any dread of it. I
doubt if you have ever wittingly set your faces
to the mist since you grew greybeards; the
desire of knowledge and the fear of the unknown
died gradually with that growth. I cannot conceive your tie to life. How much of romance
have you left? Have you still the dear fiction
that there are wondrous things beyond the west?
I am sure that long since you have forgot the
very name of Woman. She is a domestic instru-
ment between you and the dark; to escape
thither you must pass her. She fends you from
the eventual evil; you know nothing more of
her.

From this side forty your plight seems piteous,
but I dare be sworn you are happy. You are
without hopes, but you are without fears; and
you have the pleasant occupation of life.

THE LOTOS SHORE

FAR lovelier than the vale in Ida reaches this valley dreamfully towards the sea. Inland above the lesser heights rise the purple mountains faint and mystical through the gauze of dawn, barriers of the great outer world, spectral sentinels upon the peace and resignation of this nether ravine. Closed upon all sides from the vagrant foot of man, the long and gentle slope stretches through mead and woodland to the grey sands upon the shore. Day passeth after day, and night giveth place to night, but in this silent land naught moves or changes, all is eternally immutable. For day and night have we none, but one great dreamtide beneath the sun or in the shadows of the darkness. Between us and God's troubled creatures that serve Him hour by hour most dolorously yawns the wide chasm of forgetfulness. At the gate of our refuge the soul must take its farewell of sorrow, of thought, of labour, of ecstasy, of pain; for here, one and determinate, is contentment—soft, sleep-

ing, still and changeless beatitude. Away beyond
the seas, beyond the mountains, hearts burn and
wither at destiny, faint and re-arise in the sorry
fabric of life; with us still lie the rebel humours,
soft runs the placid blood, gently sinks the weary
mortal upon a divine apathy. At this sweet
low level do our lives pass smoothly in a quiet
sleep of dreams and moving fancies. The air is
tranquil and serene; from the odorous groves the
birds call musically, drooping slowly into silence;
all things, grown drowsy with ease, fall mute and
cease; full is the peace that breathes o'er the
shore of this our Lotos Land.

At the first breath of dawn in the wide heaven
above us tree murmurs to tree in the woodland,
bird calleth to bird in the close thickets, flower
noddeth to flower upon the meadows, and the
light creeps up the fells and sets the tiny brooks
alight; the hill-slants soften to the East and
the white peaks of the mountains take the
sun. Sleep shakes his wings free of us as the
day-star quivers overhead, and the quiet visions
of the night pass from the kindly darkness and
look out upon the new day through our lustrous eyes. There is no waking to the sombre
laws that once set us limits in the world; there
is no border 'twixt our dreams and our life: on
flows the level tide through waking and through
sleeping, through light and shadow, day by day and
night by night. Of old-time phantom monsters,

grisly fears, and ghostly thoughts were for our
nightly portion.   Of what be they dreaming in
the fevered world this dawn, ere eyes shall open
upon hideous life ?   Where now be those awful
memories on our Lotos Shore ?   Night hath fared
forth from us, the morning is at hand, and we
awaken with dear smiles to go dreaming anew
down the long and perfect day.   From dawn till
noon, from noon till nightfall, at the back end of
the long shore the sea washes languorously about
the hollow cliffs and open strand, cooing her
whispers in our drowsy ears.   Listen to the
voices in the lazy surf rolling in low cadences
upon the yellow beach ! So stilly, so subtly,
gather in our hearts the sounds of this silent
valley that they appear faint echoes from a distant world : a world of phantasms, a world of
shadows, a world of immaterial and exquisite
music.   Dead is all here to the jargon of distressing passions ; voiceless and vain they cry to
us for fellowship, thin jaded wraiths of another
sphere gibbering across the waste of waters—unheard, unheeded, dimly seen through misty veils.
Eyes open gently and look forth their content,
lips sigh their pleasure to the zephyrs.   There is
neither death nor life within this place of seclusion ; there is but peace that leadeth kindly to
the end.   Mortality hath here its final home, a
lodging against the darkness.   What soul can
travail in this resting-place, what poor spirit

falter at its imminent extinction? All, all is
slumbrous peace ; the bonds of the troubled flesh
are broken, the tired spirit lulls and is mute, for
this hush that broodeth continuously is death in
life, and death is the precious goal of our dim,
languid thoughts.   Here at least we have an end
of pain and jealous joy, here we have put off
the body, the weariful disguise of an aspiring
soul.   The yellow lotos on the meads hath
overmastered God's secrets and come between us
and our humanity.   No longer are we of the race
of men ; they loom in our eyes as strange and
unknown creatures in a strange and unknown hell.
The cares of them, far off, remote and inaccessible,
peer at us through the mists of oblivion—forlorn,
desperate, unintelligible shapes, mad, haggard-
eyed, lean, miserable ghosts.   In the still noontide and the stiller evening we watch them in our
visions flitting, a myriad host, about the emmets
of Time's continent—things such as once we
were.   And in them cry the voices of our past
and woful lives, reaching us yet in echoes—still,
sweet, melancholy echoes, the phantoms of a
troubled memory turned to a soothing pleasure
by the benign device of distance.   Thus weareth
the afternoon to its close.

And when the westering sun slips over the
hills and the shadows fall upon the sky, our
hearts are still undarkened, basking in the clear
sunshine of repose.   The reaches of the valley

abide in a dead calm, and the songs of bird and stream and tree hush in the dusk. Then in the twilight rises a soft voice calling us through the deepening shadows, as the allurement of a delicate love, the mirage of that earthly Desire we once held so sweet a recompence for all the pangs of living. It calls and calls across the meadows and through the thickets, summoning to rest. Here with the unvexing spirits of our long-dead desires is rest, sweet rest. And the lid of day closes over the dale, and night falls upon us clothed in our sufficient happiness. Through the darkness, the great darkness, comes no thought of care or joy, but the dewy blessing of immeasurable forgetfulness descends upon all; and life hushes but a little deeper, for here all life is but a hush. The sea washes on the beach to our listless ears, the fragrance of the ranker dells steals into our senses; we have made Time our thrall, and there is neither yesterday nor to-morrow, but merely Now. Thus rid of Time, ours is full immortality: though hour by hour and day by day we draw nearer to the waters whereon old Charon's boat floats idly waiting for the signal of a greater rest.

THE PHILOSOPHY OF THE CARESS

T is surprising to what monstrous importance the empty habit of caressing has continuously aspired. When all is considered it is surely a ridiculous item in a man's daily ritual, yet upon it hangs the whole service of woman; it is the most particular act in her worship, to abolish which would be to raise the devil at once upon our affections. I speak in a little remoteness from the whole topic, having studied these many years to regard it from a discreet distance. I do not indeed claim that I am without the influences of the passion, having in my memory a few absurdities of the past; but I have come, I think, by diligence and abstention, to an equable calm wherein the heat and glamour of this idle custom seem truly remarkable. I make no doubt that it is of our ancestry we inherit the instinct; but to accept this is to grow no wiser—is still to go marvelling that its hold upon us should be so intolerably severe. At this

late date, one would suppose, the thing would
have resigned its tenure, as we develop more perfectly into the purely intellectual. For that it is
sheerly animal is beyond all doubt, as also that
it is still a catholic taste. And yet in a manner
it is not hard to understand why it should be so
popular. In itself the world has a pleasant soothing cadence—caress—and there is besides the full
tide of song from the most ancient days, a tradition nigh irresistible. But the act itself has a
charm, an indescribable charm, which I will not
deny. I have in my mind a situation in which I
can conceive the coolest would delight. To be
within a short reach of some pretty maiden ; to
have realised her fair proportions at a glance ; to
see the rose growing in her cheeks, the eyes silent
midway 'twixt fear and joy, the lips soft, dubious,
so manifest, so imminent—there were surely but
one obvious issue from the propinquity. I am
free to confess that a fascination of this sort is
most natural. Indeed I have myself known one
between whom and me I was fain to put the table
whenever we met ; my distrust of my own resistance was so great. There was never so dainty a
creature as she appeared in her exquisite raiment,
with her admirable contour, her engaging complexion, her shining eyes of blue, her inviting lips.
Were it not for a certain timidity in her manner,
which rebuked me into a withdrawal, I would
have often ventured upon the kiss I had always in

my thoughts when I saw her ; and when I had
left I would invariably reflect upon my diffidence
with feelings of regret. I can recall that on one
occasion she—— But much has changed since
that time, and I myself have grown to take a
more philosophic view of life. It is clear then,
that the taste for the caress is still vehement ; I
can compare it to nothing so excellently as to the
desire for an intoxicant, and the effects are very
similar. You will experience a ridiculous elation,
you will grow hot, you will turn giddy of the
head, and the end will be to set up a craving. It
does not seem that a reasonable being should submit himself to this slavery of the wits.

And though its power be great the practice is
trifling. It is the view of some that this is of no
consequence ; for all pleasures being bubbles, they
say, this is no more inferior than others. It is
not my place here to appeal for the abolition of
the triviality, if that indeed were possible, but
merely to consider the thing as it is : to account
for its potency, and even in a measure to apologise
for its existence. And if you accept it as an
essential fact in human nature, the practice has a
fair claim to observance. While we have woman
with us it would seem indispensable. And woman
herself, it is obvious, serves a necessary use,
though that be little outside the indefinite pro-
longation of the race. In the common concerns
of daily living she is of no very clear advantage,

has no very secure position. There is no one, I
may conjecture, who would go the length of in-
sisting that he took any genuine pleasure in her
conversation or her manner of conduct. It is so
plainly the possibility of the caress that keeps
him in her neighbourhood, the undeniable
usufruct of her sex. Beyond this I see no gain
in the possession of her kind. To put it baldly,
this property of hers is the one reasonable apology
for her being ; all the virtues of her depend from
the performance. If we do not take her to exist
for the mere experiment of propagation—an unworthy view of her—she has been created also for
this potent though ridiculous pleasure. I am
offering no excuse for the absurdity, which is
patent, but simply acknowledging the power,
which again is in the knowledge of all. There
can be little doubt that the monotony of our
converse, with its regular and recurrent offices,
would put us to disgust of our condition, did we
not find these bubble pleasures within easy distance. Life may be a poor thing at the best, but
its distractions are near, and the madness of the
lover is one of them. It lies between us and
placid stagnation, and, though fatuous and a
derivative of the animal from which I for one
would desire to see the race emerge, is yet a factor
to be reckoned and put to service. The caress
and its congeners may often stand for a buckler
against evil days, upon which Time may fling his

shafts in vain. This is a most superlative estimate of its value, but from my knowledge I can believe it is precise. In the memory of a kiss, I am informed, men may live out their troubles. Some have pleaded, they assure me, that their lips held the fragrance of another's for a se'nnight, inspiring them upon their rounds to breast the utmost misfortune. If the testimony be true, woman has veritably a meritorious use ; and the issue of my inquiries and my thoughts has been to confirm this witness in favour of the vulgar practice.

A COLLOQUY ON THE HEARTH

T lay upon the hearth, basking in the comfortable heat, and looked at me distressfully. Such a melancholy inspired its brown eyes as seemed to question me of our common plight in this world. I could not but fancy it had endured its disappointments, had found life something of a failure, and was yet resigned to the act of living. So much the implicit silence of those eyes revealed to me.

'A thing,' said I, 'of such emotions should have a tale to tell. I cannot believe you to be the placid vehicle of a few rude instincts. You have emotions; the tears have trickled down your muzzle. Those eyes have wept; that heart has burned. Your soul has feasted on good things; you have had your moments of aspiration, your doubts, your fears, your incredulities, your pangs, your sense of loss. I, here, that address you, can claim no more. We have referred you to a lower class, but you have even the superiority of wisdom. For I sit by and

174

bicker with these thoughts, while you are content
to scrutinise me with your calm, indifferent gaze.
We fret and fume; yours is the peace of knowledge.'

The creature put its nose into my hand.

'And with your doubts,' I said, 'you have
also an extreme faith.   Do you question, I
wonder, your tedious service?   Have you ever
taken a disgust for your calling?   Was there
never a whimsey in your head, that you should
quit your servitude and go yourself set up for a
gentleman of leisure?   You have your wits—
they are of the sharpest—and yet you will live in
an humble obedience, pleased with your master's
pleasure, sad in his sorrow, hungry when he is
anhungered, mad with him, too; with him, too,
wicked and perverse.   It has not been an easy
bondage, and you have ever discovered a sensitive
spirit, cowed by his frown, humble in his disfa-
vour.   And yet you have never relinquished him;
if all else have fallen away, you only have re-
mained.   Is it of your great heart alone you keep
this fidelity? or is it also that you lack desire—
that as you are resigned to life, so also are
you to friendship?   You are our great Exemplar
of constancy; it is you, and you only, death finds
watching.'

It blinked its eyes and yawned at the fire.

'I wonder at your patience,' I said.   'I know
your ways; your fluent vitality is familiar to me,

You come of a brave, sound stock, no whit below my own, and have retained the primal vigour. I have never seen you tire at your work; your tongue lolls from your mouth, you slobber at the jaws—but these are merely superficial signs of a pleasant excitement. You are upon your legs all day; you revel in action; to be up and about is your one delight. But you will sit for hours at the pinch of duty; you will keep guard as no human sentinel is able. No restlessness irks you. You will look into the fire and be still, if it be your master's wish. You may be bored an hundredfold, and will never declare it. You are a miracle of courteous tolerance.'

The creature wagged its tail.

'Whence,' I asked, 'have you that sweet cheerfulness which seems to sit so at ease upon you? Your wistful eyes proclaim you an inheritor of evil; you have been upon the rack of this tough world with all of us. Bitter have been your sorrows, doubtless; sharp your pains. And you can have few ambitions, but a meagre prospect— the satisfaction of an instant appetite, the hope of a caress. From day to day there is no great change in your life; your round is surely as dull and immemorable as ours. Never a pleasure presses itself upon you uninvited; evils make their board with you. You have the fear of death, and yet you are merry withal. In a twinkling you have thrown off your troubles,

and put on your dancing humour.   Fun sparkles
in your face.   You watch my mood and fall in
with it.   Am I pleased to laugh, you too will
wag your tail.   There is no distress you cannot
forget in order to sport with me.   There is no
gaiety like yours, no joyous abandonment in
Nature so precipitate, so notable.   The world is
your prison.   How have you beautified and
adorned it with contentment ! '

The creature stretched its nose upon its paws,
and slept.

'And your philosophy,' I said, 'how marvellous !   I could swear none other has so mastered
the secrets of conduct.   You live opportunely
with your environment, and have adapted yourself to this archaic muddle we call the world.
For there is none that can obliterate as you do.
You can pass out of the present and be still on
the moment.   Whatever trials surround you, by
whatsoever menaces you are begirt, however sad
your temper, you have but to stick your muzzle
to the floor and are at once in oblivion.   Sweet
is this happy refuge of sleep and quietude.   You
have the keys of peace ; for hourly in this still
abstraction are you soothed and renewed.   Here
—here is your lesson to mankind.   For, howso-
ever great the tribulation, a little space will prevail against it.   All things swing into balance
again ; Nature disturbed resumes her equipoise.
And if we shall be content to tarry a little in

M

forgetfulness, as an animal hibernates through
the severities of an unruly season, we shall return
to the norm of our lives.   By what divine guid- .
ance have you put in practice a truth as yet but
partly revealed to us?'

The creature growled in its dreams.

'It is so,' said I: 'you have also your passions.
Derived from a savage and honourable blood,
your hot instincts have been refined and
chastened by the years; but they are still lively
within you.   Yours is no craven heart, nor
have you given yourself over to undue sentiment.   Pity you can feel, and affection, but yet
upon occasion you can be fierce and passionate.
Your smooth benevolence comes from no lack of
spirit.   Ay, you have the fire of the prime, as
you have the energy.   And your muscles are not
flabby with inaction.   There is, in truth, no
decadence in you; you have preserved your vital
faculties unbroken, but only tempered.   You can
fly out in rage when it is needful; and there is
no wrath more merciless than yours, as there is
no judgment more discreet.   You can define the
evil, and will visit upon it your justest indignation.'

The creature woke and watched me.

'You are of iron nerve,' I said, ' of resolute will,
of a strong and enduring frame; you have a full
knowledge of life, and have composed yourself to
its accidents.   You are a boon companion; yours

is the most soothing fellowship.   You have the finest sympathies, the largest affections.   These qualities are of the essence of our earthly desires. How have you contrived them ?   What be your thoughts ?   What passes in your mind as you regard me now with steadfast and searching eyes? Were you put in communion with me here, what voice would you find, to what secret would you admit me ?'

The creature rose and looked at me ; in its eyes it strove hard with its thoughts ; it whined, and licked my hand.

HER PICTURE

THOUGH her picture has been with me but these few short weeks it has so crept into my past that I can conceive not the room without it. I had not thought myself solitary here before, but now should her face vanish from my wall I were indeed in ashes. From its place in the still corner it looks out upon me through the day with eyes of full hazel, wistfully; and at times the firelight flickering in the golden brown of her hair and o'er her close unassailable lips turns them to a vivid appearance of life. And yet it is not in this demure mood of gravity I know her best, which is in a manner strange to her custom, at most a rare and passing exhibition of her thoughtfulness. If you should see this exquisite portrait you would proclaim her of a tender seriousness, one that had caught some knowledge of the world's travail, nor learnt to smile at it, though the gift of joyous blood ran in her veins. You would misjudge her did you so imagine her. For she has no unwholesome gravity, is not oppressed by outer woes, suffers not vicari-

ously beyond a woman's habit, is blithe and
jocund, nods at her own poor troubles merrily,
and meets fortune with a negligence of uncommon
grace.   There is none other whom her dainty
gaieties so become.   She has in truth sedater
moments as in this picture; but I am assured
that her eyes go no further than the eyes of her
happy sisters, her lips whisper nothing more.
This visage of shy solemnity is not most notable
of her, and yet I love its mute expression even as I
love her speaking face.   Her winsome smile in life
possesses all my idle hours; her sober gaze from
out the mellow canvas moves me to draw a little
nearer to her through my daily work.   Her gaiety
is sweet to me, yet somehow I prefer her picture
to be grave and quiet.   To have her laughing
ever in my face were to wince at a certain callous
apathy of the cold paint.   I suffer the common
tragedies of mortality day by day; my humours
vary with the shifting hours; anon I am in pain
or sorrow; and that she should be witness with
her smile were distasteful to me, as it were to her
own pitiful self.   And so as I bend to my work she
looks down upon me hour by hour, peaceful and
softly earnest, till the peace and earnestness of
her presence have entered also into the possession
of my spirit.

This picture is now my dearest treasure, a
function of my heart, as integral a part of myself
as are my constant thoughts and fancies.   The

gross accidents of life step between me and her
daily, but her picture nought may assoil; it
abides with me always, a gracious guardian above
the reach of chance or time.   Though she herself
should fade from my experience (which God in
His grace forbid!) I have her here still watching
me with a most kind regard.   Those lustrous
eyes, fashioned of raw paint, informed with light
and life, keep ward upon the world in which I
move, so steadfastly that I could think they
follow my diurnal course, and at my failures will
grow wet with tears.   And yet her own sweet
eyes, I am persuaded, have never wept for me,
whose servitude is but a vain reiterated tribute to
her loveliness.   To bow before her is the common
lot; man's adoration and her beauty are two
correlatives of fate ; the one is born and moveth
with the other.   Many there be that live upon
her smile; there is but one that hath taken her
picture for his heart.   That soft face speaking
from the wall has grown to be my conscience ;
most often has it detached me from the society of
rude thoughts and ruder companions.   When I
am most errant and most evil of mind I have but
to look up and read her delicate glance to rid me
of my inmost devil.   At such times I shut my
lips against my babble, and listen to her low
voice through the boisterous talk, bethinking me
how unworthy am I of so delicious a communion.
She in her counterfeit shares with me my

graver thoughts, though she herself has suffered me no entrance into her interior feelings. From her outward conduct to me, who am a mere atom in her pleasant circle, she would appear to be very human, full of light, heedless, dainty whims. I should consider, did I judge her so, that her mind runs little on sad phantasies. Her customs are so joyous and unrestrained, and she bears upon her face the marks of a great and smiling innocence. This behaviour doth belie her.

Still I keep company with her graver picture, though her pretty frolics thrill me through and through. I come from the vivid flesh to the breathing image on the wall. They are both real to me, the same in diverse moods: the one as I know her best, the other as I should know her worthiest could I but look, clandestine, into her soul. These twain resemblances mirror her full nature, comprising the sentient round: the one in life with her brimming eyes of mirth, the other with her sedate and chastened looks watching me about my room. How near had I grown to her were I the licensed intimate of this grave mood in life! Ofttimes have I caught but a fleeting glimpse of it when the laughter ebbed from her dimples, and it has shown me in a flash how far I stood from one who locked her secret thoughts so closely. 'It is thus I have seen you at sweet intervals,' I cry to her picture; 'it is thus I would have you always in my room. Yet

it is not thus,' I cry, 'I would have you always
live your pretty life.' For that soft countenance
was not born for tears. Time, indeed, shall bring
it these moments of awe: pray God, but rarely!
Smiles are fitter to her need than sombre meditation. That fragile, exquisite life shall be wrecked
upon no austere denial. Let the shadow pass!
It is nothing in the sunlight.

Thus have I come to read the changing humours
of this pictured face, which often when I fix my
gaze upon it seems to be instinct with gracious
humanity. It is so perfect in its delicate flesh
that (methinks) it needs but a little to break
through the rigid surface of the canvas and
descend to very life. Immured and pent within
the smooth dead medium breathes the soul of
one, real and palpitant; and beneath the eyelids thoughts seem to burn and glow till I have
wondered that the lashes flicker not and the lids
close not at my ardent gaze. And when in the
twilight I look through dim and half-closed
vision I can see that soft white bosom slowly
rise; the brocade sparkles, the lips quiver and
part, the eyes open from their dreaming, the
aureate hair waves in the breath of the evening.
She seems to dissolve into warm flesh and come
out to me with a sudden cry of welcome. Should
she step forth, I think I should greet her with no
surprise, so implicit am I in her constant presence: yet a little timorously, lest in her con-

tinuous guardianship she had acquired a distaste for my inferior ways.   And yet I know that she would only break into smiles, and that I should but feel the familiar clasp of her hands, but see that alluring curve of her mouth.   As I have ever been to her so should I then be: a unit in a multitude, one but as others, used with no special care or individual attention.

GROTESQUE, precarious, defiant, here stands this temple of the human soul, the house of infinite pains, the plaything of organic change, the masterpiece of God. Erect from a trivial foundation, framed of a mysterious stuff unknown, insecure, desperately resolute, fulfilled of gay bravery, obnoxious to all general vicissitudes, it fronts the baser principalities of earth, unbending, unafraid. In its passage out of the void its home into the void its bourne, it holds a brief tenure of the world, the mark of multiform and multitudinous antagonists. It is transfigured from the worthless dust; and 'twixt that state of precedent nothingness and this stage of delicate life lies a divine handicraft, the ever-recurrent miracle, which should you fathom you were come to the skill of God. Pallid and frail, composite of vain and sluggish elements that blow about a windy world, it has uprisen to such a glory, has touched such an eminence, has assumed so fine a property, that now it moves the noblest visibility on earth.

From the hour of its conception to its moment of eternal rest it swaggers stoutly against brave old Time, eager to wrest some short and meagre privilege. All the coarse and stridulous creatures of inferior creation come out against it, arrayed as one to lay it in its kindred ashes. All evils have their way with it; day by day and year by year a myriad demons claw and fret it. Earth unchains her monstrous horrors against it: the vile universe joins in a sordid bond to thrust it back upon its Maker. Out of the deeps, from the shallows, upon the flat, in cloister, upon open, out of space and all eternity issues the hot breath of their wrath upon it, this poor, slim, tremulous continent of life, the latest-born of God, the final achievement of the æons. Earth has no trial, hell has no torture, ruthless enough to inflict upon this fabric. Fragile, weak, perishable, sensitive of all, it stands subjective to the wild hand of Nature, piteous, unpitied, terrible, undeterred, supreme still over its vehement adversaries, indefatigable, steadfast, tolerant, and debonair, prolific and populous, the most eminent and sanest apparition upon the whole globe.

Thus tenaciously existent it endures, the keeper of that superior soul that is ourself. And, derivative of earth, while still our guardian, it smacks yet of its own lowly constituents. By it we have our being—this is its finest service —and with it we are ever in tumultuous war.

From end to end of its swift course it is ever in
our bonds and we in its; now the one in servitude, anon the other. Twin with the spirit in .
being, it battles ceaselessly for the lordship: now
the slave and abject, now the imperial task-
master.   Dumb, blind, insensate, it yet lends
eyes, ears, and intellectual vision to the soul.   It
is a clog, a heavy burden to trail us in the mire,
turning to clay its own inhabitant; yet by its
means we move, aspire, and pray.   Anon is it
servile to the spirit's uses, anon it slips the yoke
and bolts for ruin.   It descends upon abasement;
its haunts are animal and low; it is fain to
grovel; it is dull and somnolent; it would keep
us perforce in company with our lowermost
agnates, after the likeness of which it is fashioned.
Yet in itself it is the material conduit of a
thousand lofty feelings; not one fine thought or
noble fancy but has run through its vile and
wonderful channels.   We are its subject and its
debtor; we are its contemptuous over-lord.   Here
have we our home appointed us: herein we watch
its growth, its lapses, its wayward courses, its
eccentric, unlovely, and most horrid humours;
and when it fails we fail in synchronism, clinging
to it in despair, calling upon it as ourself, mourn-
ful and disconsolate, shamelessly tenacious of it,
fain to grope a way from out it, all ungrateful
for its hospitable sanctuary, weeping and praying
for an immortality this thing has never craved.

And I beseech you, when from your pulpits you behold the helpless faces of the sinners moving to your wrath and bowing in the trouble of your displeasure—I beseech you to remember these meritorious benefits. This edifice of dust and passion, whereof you too are in the bonds, should plead with you for mercy; a voice in it should cry out upon your clamant indignation, asking a little pity by reason of its own malignant composition. Here stands the body humbled before the magnificent soul, itself the plea for its own pardon. To the one falls the burden of the long day; to the other is meeter that divine communion to which you would exhort us. If, indeed, we stand between God and the brute, pardon us a little that we divide our interests unevenly. We have no right to make exact comparisons; doubtless we are gone astray with the body in which we lie, our close and narrow prison-house, our exigent and sleepless tyrant. I would have you to reflect how ceaseless is its vigilance, how distressing its penalties, and, recalling the long slavery of our fathers, to stay your denunciation of the habit in ourselves. We have been well-instructed in the truth, and the blood of goodwill is in us; the more part of us have set out to be careful of the right. From our mothers at birth we took the gift of excellent intention, and were framed for honour in her eyes, full of promise and hope. I dare guess

there be few of us that have not made some
gallant endeavour to deal honourably by our
heritage, to cleave unto the better way, to spur .
the dull body from its baser tastes. Out of its
ignorant eyes the child looked upon life and
spake scorn of its wickedness, marvelling at the
lapses of the half-divine. Surely therein the image
of God was come to dishonourable uses, his
trust betrayed, his hopes foregone, his faith
shipwrecked, his pride swallowed in abysmal
degradation. But soon the facile-growing body
would outlap the soul; slowly the effort ceased,
the wonder died, and the infernal prison-house,
our fort and garrison, compact, inexorable, closed
round the struggles of its fearful tenant. Life
then, you must consider, took an added shade of
horror; for he that was most surely half-divine
was nought now but the fell animal of his
ascendants, pleased with its pleasures, hedged by
its afflictions, stayed by its limits. The iron
mould, growing ever more rigid, held in its core
that nobler part incarcerate. And this iron flesh,
our kind and goodly servitor, at once our gaoler
and our bodyguard, is the blind subject of its
own strict laws; which we too thus come to follow
and obey. And this body which is death is the
sole vehicle of life.

A PLEA FOR INCONSTANCY

CONSTANCY has always received an improper meed of praise at the hands of the moralists. At the best it is a dull virtue, of no special allurements for the young and beautiful, fitter for dusty age, and no doubt a comfort in the grave. It would be easy to tell the advantages of this respectable quality, which, in truth, lie upon the surface, and make a pretty show at first sight; but its adherent failings are even more eminently visible upon deeper consideration. Constancy is the fruit of a social convenience, the heirloom from a time when solid comforts went for more than an exact delight in the offerings of Nature. The ambition of the barbarians that once we were was to live in perfect ease, with as few distractions from the engrossing appetites as possible, and with as small a spiritual reflection as might be. Constancy was to these the happiest expedient, being in a manner a moral assurance that in regard to one concern of life at least they were to be at no trouble or expense. But though the invention of the virtue was felicitous in the extreme, its tradition to our days is not wholly as welcome. Constancy, to speak plainly, is a most stagnant virtue, and one that should reflect little credit upon its exhibitor. It is one that is achieved with ridiculous ease, consumes little time, and occupies few faculties. It makes no call upon the intellect nor upon the soul; it is neither discreet nor voluntary: but is in the main a blind, mute instinct as mechanical and uninspiring as the tenacious grip of a lobster or the unreasoning attachment of a limpet. Two such primordial creatures duly juxtaposed will grow together as a matter of course, lacking the natural impetus to wander from each other. The horizon of the constant is limited, their environment has narrow bounds; they themselves are sparingly percipient and massively lethargic. So that it would seem that those who cultivate this false virtue affect the distinctive quality of an inferior organisation. Constancy is the cheap possession of the mediocre. It is followed by its adherent as naturally as the mule will chase the carrots dangling in his blinkers, or the tame horse follow after his own nose. It needs no incentive to pursue, no more than does a wheel to run down an incline or a dog to go baying at the noises in the air. It is the inherited habit of the dull and docile to be faithful; and to break through this habit is no more

possible than for a machine to have a mind of its
own.   It is nothing to the credit of the train
that once set a steaming it keeps to the appointed
lines; but should it take to leaping the hedges,
there were some original spirit here.   Constancy
is the obvious, the commonplace, the mechanical,
the necessary, if you will (for it is doubtless indispensable to the work of the world); but it is
singularly unhandsome and unromantic.

Constancy is the sepulture of admiration, and
has, indeed, an ugly look of death itself; while
inconstancy, on the other hand, is always alert and
vital.   To take the surest pleasure in the world's
many lovely possessions we must have inconstant
hearts, which shall find rest nor stop in no one
thing, but keep perpetually astir.   A protracted
devotion to a single object is a reckless extravagance of time and soul; and there is no more dismal fate than thus to fall into an infatuated absorp-
tion, and become heedless of other opportunities
of joy.   The plight of one who had put such a wall
to his affections were deplorable, for he would be
no partner with Time in the eternal changes.
Constancy, it may be, runs deep and strong, but
it runs also narrow; whereas inconstancy gads in
a broad stream, indifferently ecstatic.   Its bed is
here to-day and there to-morrow, and the day
after somewhere else; none can foretell its eccentric
courses; for there is but one thing certain—that
it will flow through the best and choicest pastures.

Inconstancy is the dilettante, constancy the poor professional content with the humdrum round. The one is a brave rogue, the other but a sober-coated citizen. Life full of faithfulness were too puritan, too dogmatic, too grey and reputable; its little infidelities give to it a dainty colour and a jaunty air. The constant soul answers but to one strain and is insensible of foreign melodies; the inconstant has an ear for the newest and rarest music. The one is a connoisseur, the other an ignoramus. The world lies open to inconstancy; constancy keeps the gate locked upon itself, and in its moments of self-distrust is minded to lose the key and thank God for a good deed. Should it be tempted for an instant out of its melancholy fidelity, it will withdraw from the beguiler precipately and go to grass again in all humility and penitence.

But it is possible to excuse the inconstant on somewhat more material grounds. They live in accordance with the laws of natural change as with the regulations of their own being. It would be an affront to one's personal design to pick but one of several attractions. Nature, a worthy exemplar and pattern, is immutably fickle, and be assured it is against her wish and precept if we alone are still and changeless. She has an elegant dislike to monotony, and expends herself in dodging it; and she has informed us with the same shifting tastes. We weary of a dress, we weary of a

fare, of a scene, of a company; and why should
it be for a reproach that we weary also of a
passion? It is only an absurd tradition that
discriminates between these different pleasures.
And, in a word, to be done with logic, those who
obey their own fancies in this matter, and not an
austere ordinance, will find their plainest justifica-
tion in the issues of their conduct. Inconstancy,
be it known now and for all time, is the one
superior of death. Our deepest pains come of
long fellowship and plethoric association : these
will the inconstant avoid. We do not mourn
the unknown nor the indifferently acquainted ; so
too a passing admiration will entail merely a
passing regret. Some are crushed to the earth by
loss as by an intolerable burden ; these are the
prosaic faithful : and this is their reward—they
go down into the dust of their own sorrow. But
the inconstant may endure many such trials without discomfiture ; having paid their respects to
the past they have still the future. They take off
their hats to trouble, but are on more intimate
terms with happiness. Day by day they come
freshly to their pleasure, as the bee to its work,
under no obligation to attend one flower rather
than another, with no regret for the last if the
next will serve as well, and with no silly vows of
permanent devotion. Life is most insecure ; it
needs that Love also should be.

THE SHADOW ON THE YEAR

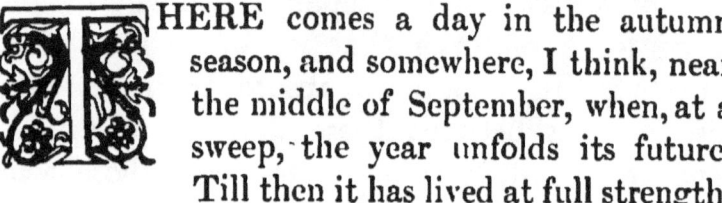

THERE comes a day in the autumn season, and somewhere, I think, near the middle of September, when, at a sweep, the year unfolds its future. Till then it has lived at full strength, ominous of no failure through all its changes, with no menacing *memento mori:* with no doubt, no question, of its own absolute sufficiency. Virile even in its excesses, it has laid with an easy air the eternal forces of dissolution; so that we in its bosom have grown to forget them. So much of seeming power has there been in its lavish performance that we have never considered defeat. Yet upon this day of humiliation it is come, and the strong year bows to its mortality with silent resignation. What an abject to-day, and how proud but yesterday! It is strange the discovery should be so swift and so sudden; it comes in a flash to the year and those that trust in it. There is no quiet ebbing of the full life. The tide stands still, turns in the moment, and behold it racing seaward! This day is surely known to all of us. You remember

that hour in the sudden gloaming when the miasma
of the autumn crept through your nostrils.
Last night it was a full moon, and looking from
my window I saw the stars flicker out, and felt
the cool air enwrap me.   It was summer then,
and I had the dreams of a summer night; there
was a warmth in the blood of the earth, and its
smile was sweet and gracious.   One could lean
over and listen to the year's fresh confidences; one
saw its young thoughts upon its face.   Nature was
unsecretive, buoyant, overbearing.   To-night she
is grown older, and her age is on her sober visage.
A little ago, as I passed into my garden to the
roses, the dusk fell and I stumbled among the flower
beds.   A mist rose quickly from the quiet earth,
and there was the savour of decay in my throat.
There were roses here last night: I watched them
from my window dipping in the breeze.   But now
I cannot find them; perhaps it is the dusk.
Surely last night there were birds in the elms and
the sweetbriar.   I vow it was a thrush I heard
calling to the moon for the lack of a nightingale.
Now there is silence; the dreary mist is creeping
higher, and I see the newly lighted street-lamps
dimming in the haze.   A chill is mounting in my
bones.   The tide is running seaward; the year
is persuaded of death.

At this unexpected hour of her defeat is all
evil triumphant.   In one moment, as it were, the
year sickens, and conscious of her destiny, falls

to thinking on the grave. Through the breach
in her fine vitality rise abysmal vapours of the
underworld—out of the patient earth the fog
and the deadly chill; nor shall anything prevail
against them longer. Unto Nature is revealed
now her own impotence, and she must henceforth
go with her hand to her heart; stricken with eld
she must limp forward to her tomb. It is long
months since we knew her young and debonair,
when each of her movements was tremulous with
vigour, vivid with significance. How vain she
was, how riotous, how merry! She did not spare
her thews in the whirl, but drained all the
pleasures. And yet she has worn the same gay
front into her fuller maturity; she has been at
one pitch till this collapse. And we have excused
this extravagance, holding her justified by the
grace of her very joyousness. Where are they
now, those vivacious measures and that noble
vanity? See this pitiful creature choking in the
damp shadows, and take heed unto yourself. For
our lives have been enclosed in hers; and her
abasement, is it not also ours? We have laughed
with her and have danced with her; with her too
shall we not weep and become the poor ghosts of
our younger selves? Nay, though we would not,
we are so constrained; our blood has lost the
quality of youth. The splendour has faded from
the fabric of our dream, from the world is gone
the charm that once held us intent upon the

nearest pleasure. It is not only that your body
carries the marks of another year, but one might
say a certain elasticity of the mind dies year by
year with Nature. You will not resume your
occupations comfortably to-night. Do you think
there is not a tinge of sadness in your laughter
over your favourite humourist? Has not your
study an air of melancholy? Your pictures
speak of the vanity of this passing life. From
your shelves a thousand still voices of your books
summon you to the thought of final rest. To
what end is this infinite trouble? Of a truth you
are a weary soul fighting for you know not
whether good or evil. In your accustomed chair
your thoughts flow inwards, and you see the
tissue of desires and aims you call yourself. If
you can find in this moment one worthy aspiration, one feeling other than of clay, then shall
you find the night a little clearer, the year a little
younger. But your poignant introspection will
perceive the weariness and the folly and the
vanity of being. Your soul is cold and clammy;
you think it on the brink of death, and cry out
upon the horror of your creation. How meanly
selfward now do all your habits show! how tire-
some your slender virtues! how misspent your
indulgences! It is but a few weeks since you had
the disposition to pride yourself on life as a very
sweet benevolence of God. Then you were sure
of your footway—saw in it a swift, short path to

golden gates. You mounted on your brave
ambitions and soared to pinnacles, doubting not
the good of them. Have you no questionings .
now, when one by one your stars have sailed into
the mist? Should you ride now so high as those
month-old thoughts, would you tremble and
despair at the mortality of your office? would you
suffer of surfeit and weariness? It would seem so
on this grey autumn evening.

But perhaps you will not have these untoward
thoughts. Perhaps these changes are but the
prelude of divers new delights, and your chair is
no seat of melancholy, but a place to forecast the
corporeal pleasures of the winter. You may
dwell upon the rich charnel colours with a delicate thrill. You have the secret of survival, so,
and are the proper denizen of this world, seeing
your correspondence with Nature is so perfect.
In truth it is an unwholesome spirit in which to
take her decadence, which, since it has recurred
through æons, must be nobly wise. Is it so?
Rots she towards perfection year by year? And
is the whole universe mutable to a supreme
glory?

It is a trifle changes us. A wind swaggering
down the street has blown the drift into rags,
and I see my stars again. They are still white
and shining.

NEÆRA'S HAIR

IEWED with a quiet judgment, as it were in the placid observation of art, I cannot affect a genuine passion for her hair. Its intrinsic worth is of the highest, I acknowledge, and it would go upon the market at a notable price. But, to be honest, I have never taken fire save at the touch of something very human, and the absolute or the ideal, however consummate, I have always reckoned in the very coldest values. The sheer perfection of a form or colour, the exquisite achievement of some independent and impersonal beauty, has always seemed to me desolate and uninspiring. It is the easiest affair to execute marmoreal contours, and to follow them with the eye is to get only the integral interpretations of sense ; but relate them to a human soul, and the very devil is in your emotions. Of themselves the tresses of a woman's hair discover no particular charm, but may be simulated in a score of factories. There is, to be

sure, a certain distinction in colours, as there are
also degrees of fineness and variations of abundance; but properties of this sort away from the
human subject are ineloquent and ineffectual.
Were it not for her own rare beauty and the
individual framework of her sex, I fear Neæra's
hair would be of little moment in my life;
whereas it is now the supreme end and finish of
her loveliness, for which I profess a taste something unwarrantable and very inordinate.

'God,' I have said, while riveted upon the confusion of her face, 'contrived three wonders in
this creature, woman: the one her eyes; her long
and slender outline for the second; and—to crown
all—her hair. The rest, maybe, He rendered by
some deputy.' The thought is a superfluous
blasphemy, the merest ecstasy of contemplation,
in no wise the issue of my calmer moments. As
at a sober distance from her presence I resolve
within myself the complex riddle of my feelings
for her, I can see now how unessential, how
immaterial, is that one grace of hers that takes
me to the upper heights of passion. Her hair is
the most idle accident of her composition, an
after-thought in her design, a supererogant fancy,
nothing warm nor intimate, imposed upon the
full, rich body of her breathing humanity. All
other parts of her have part in her; her hair
alone is distressingly exterior. I can hardly
imagine there is one freer than herself to the

mercy of tempestuous and aëry humours. I suppose she is more supremely sensitive to her own
thoughts than any of her sex since Eve : the
slightest flutter of her heart flashes on the instant
in her eyes, and thrills through her delicate
flesh. More sensations flit over her changing
features than you would credit to the feelings
of an hour. Her expressions are her soul, and
she herself is an oblation to the visual passions.
But in all those outward offices her hair has no
part ; the passions in full cry sweep through
her, leaving it unruffled. It is extrinsic and im-
particular, the veriest appanage to an unerring
mirror of her inner self, of a cold essential beauty,
changeless, subservient, gestureless, and dead.
There is no fancy nor mood in her soul but
twinkles a moment in her eyes, which are a
record surer than might be devised of science.
Each mute thought, demure or wild, rebellious or
serene, leaps in a dart to the surface of that blue,
flashes and drowns in those deep and silent wells.
Nor is there a strenuous emotion that spares her
slender frame. I have seen Fear break from her
eyes, pass, and run trembling down her body.
Disdain has gleamed through those enchanted
windows, and quivered on her fastidious shoulders.
From those clear deeps Anger has sprung forth
upon me, and her bosom has rocked to its frail
foundations. And there too I have watched
Love circling as the great lights dancing on a

summer sea.　There never lived on earth a creature of such rare poise.

And her long tresses sleep quietly upon her. head.　From all these fascinating exhibitions of herself they stand apart, dumb sentinels on her loveliness.　I could admit no glory in them separate from her, and of God's three gifts they are the least of note.　And yet they stir me as though they were the prime factors in her beauty.　To gaze upon her hair is to break the last bonds of my senses, and to set my heart crying in the night.　The lustrous brown, with its swift passages of gold, sits demure upon a dainty brow, soft, wreathing, and all-fragrant. Ten thousand wavering threads go in and out together, burning and shining and flickering on her head.　Her hair caresses her; it runs in a company of myriads, it curves in innumerable tiny arcs, it droops in a multitude of intertwined festoons; it rises in slow curls, it falls in minute and tremulous cascades; it is of infinite complexity, of manifold audacity.　And on a day when the warm summer gusts are chasing through the woods I have seen it, free of its catches, stirring in the wind, a stream of fire in the sun's eye.　At such a time it wakes into life and blows to the air.　It is as vital then as the gay features of her face; at each breath it swerves, and it tosses; it riots with the wind; it runs atremble down the breezes.　It keeps high holiday against heaven, and leaps, a merry frolic, to the sky. Ah, then is it instinct with life and light. Then is she bound with a cowl of gold : a hood of motley gold—gold upon her head and gold upon her shoulders, dancing gold about her arms and bosom.

One confidence contents me in Neæra's hair. So tranquilly it rests on her pretty head, that it will suffer no thought of change. It shall abide against the press of Time, when all else fails. Years shall not touch it, nor filch any fragrance from those coils. In the face of Death shall this fine grace be left her : change shall bereave her of her eloquent form ; the eyes shall narrow and grow dim ; but untarnished, unimpaired, surely that golden hair shall abide through all decay.

'THE VOICE OF STRANGE
COMMAND'

THERE is a call in that white star luminous in the south this midnight. In it, hanging silent over Africa, I hear the still voices of the world ringing from zone to zone to invoke the sleeper from his dreams. Its clear, pellucid light is a reproach against the indolent round of my life. It was not wont of old time thus to be regarded by a contemplative race of men; not as a pleasant problem for the philosopher, not as the darling figure of the rhymer, nor for the signal awe of the worshipper. It was a lure and a bait then to our fathers' zeal of adventure, an incessant trumpet in the placid heaven, calling to exploration of the earth's mysteries. Serene, benignant, it yet holds for me to-night an echo of those voices. Four-square to the four quarters of the world I seem to see it from my drowsy street, erect, vigilant, the spy of God's handi-work, the sentinel of a roaring earth. Heaven! what voices cry in my blood this night! How the new time fades and vanishes, leaving me the plain, bold guest of the past ! Rude, ungenerous Nature screams for my life, and I greet her claim with blows and laughter. The thunderous surge is booming in my ears and the ethereal touch of the mists is on my face ; shall I not shake my fist at the sky ? I hear the pulse of feet, and the wrack drives about me ; dry clashes my harness ; there is champing of horses : let me engage with a watchword on my lips. Here is the splendour of battle ; charge home for chivalry. The drowsy villas pass from my sight ; and lo ! the broad moon over a barren waste and wide confusion. Are not the roaring and the yelling as music ? O the fever of those noises, the glory of those spirits, rampant and clamorous ! I have set the winds to shriek. I am betwixt the devil and the blasts. Stars and glories float before me out of the illimitable. My soul sings at the approach of peril ; my heart is the heart of the universe— at one with it. I am afire to sail the world around, and fall upon the most golden adventures.

These are sounds and visions of the romance of the earth, the madness of yonder falling star, in the eye of which is no peace. Yet is the potency of its invitation paling. Generation by genera- tion does Nature swagger less and her vaunted prospect dwindle. When the earth was young and gallant her legions were indomitable, our will was a poor reed to hers. She had no pity for us then,

as now she has not, and was unsparing in her cruel
attentions. At that time to appear in bravery
before her was to disappear in a twinkling. Beyond all question she was a villainous acquaintance then; and would be so now but that her
times are accomplished. She has retained her
rancours but can only spit them at us, for we
have put her to the dust and ride roughshod
over her body. She is nothing less vicious,
nothing less wanton than of old, but indubitably
her dominion has been curtailed, the sphere of
her barbarous rule has shrunk. In her youth the
world had one neck for her, so supreme was her
outrageous sovereignty. Man had then no need
of an incitement to confront her, for she leered at
him hourly in his daily emprises. It would have
been as impossible to step out of her way as to
deny her authority; she dogged the poor wretch
persistently, played with him a little, jeered or
frowned at him upon her pleasure, and in the end
despatched him evilly. There has been no mark
upon time so notable, so deplorable, as this of
our unnatural stepmother; and, if you view our
attainments in this connection, how shall we
appear to you ' a little breed'? To have tamed
this monster, now for the better part within
blinkers, is no unworthy service, and comes of
good blood. In what quarter is she not worsted,
though fighting still? The sons of those that
perished by her are scattered abroad to their

vengeance, choking her back upon her haunches, maiming and lacerating her in a thousand places. The reverse is so complete, indeed, that I have it in my mind to commiserate her; there is some sort of tragedy in her case. Upon all sides have they risen against her, penetrating to the hinder-parts of the north, to the womb of the east where the day is born, to the white bones of the south, to the red west, to the hot and palpitant heart of the earth. In arms cap-a-pie they have raided all her quarters. Who can stand against this new power of darkness, Man? Weaklings, the virgin forests yield him their honour. Mountain and plain and their swarming tenants are to him sullen captives. He is a ravisher of the fairest, a thief, a cut-purse on old Earth's highway, a pirate, a most indefensible and monstrous libertine. He is putting all things under his feet, and it is but now and then his abjects break away for a passage of freedom; as when the main snaps its bridle and rolls over him. It is thus he atones for his ancient servitude; it is thus he is become regnant over all.

But Nature takes long a-dying; in a hundred parts she still disputes the end with all her old virulence, and it is a summons to the closing struggle I hear in yonder star. In a little the voices will have ceased and dreamful ease be our only portion: that is why the call rings so clearly to-night, mingling with all the sounds of time departed. But has, then, Nature really no further hope? Has she no surprises for us? Having slain and coffined her, shall we have taken the measure of the universe? Or, infinite as Fate, will she ever hold strange facts to which from age to age we must adjust ourselves? Shall there never be peace? And will the gross creature rise and confound us with greater wonders, and fight with her claws to the end? At least for our lessening romance shall be left man's wayward soul and his wicked imaginings. These shall go to the tourney.

CONCERNING A GRIMACE

AM unable to understand what possessed her that she puckered her face so wantonly. Ere that one act she had my sincerest homage, and but a sapient procrastination detained me from an open betrayal at her feet. I held her to be adorable beyond the common lot of women, and would have gone out of my way to thrust this faith down another's throat, even while prohibiting him from a devotion in keeping. I admit that my intentions wavered, for a man has the liberty of his manhood, and is not bound to dethrone himself at a glance. Yet I considered her, in all, so perfect an achievement as to constitute a universal challenge; and my satisfaction in her beamed in my tolerant regard of others less fortunate. She had the air of a mystery, for one thing; and it is but those we cannot plumb that draw us. For my own part I believe that the measure of one's affection is the profundity of one's ignorance. Then her talk had a certain sweetness incomparable to the accents of her

inferior sisters. The toss of her head, though
but a trick at the best, I had a fancy to see in
my mistress; it was pretty and an exquisite irritation to my fellows whom I kept from her company. 'You shall learn,' I would say to myself,
'to wriggle at my better fortune. This pretty
creature with her tricks is for me.' I desired
their envy. There was that about her mouth,
moreover, cultivated in me an outrageous appetite, which I doubt not I could have contained
but a little longer, had she not put me to shame
by this one terrible performance of her features.
For the moment I had relegated her to the company of some poor fool to whom her feminine
chatter was wisdom, who lived upon the sight of
her for weeks, and took it as an honour did I say
she had spoken of him. There is in such a crude
juvenility as of a younger time than ours, when
men took the smiles of women for their laws.
How impossible a philosophy in this wiser age,
which has allotted each his proper place! But
for the nonce I was content to watch his sudden
despatch of colour, his foolish elation, his silly
melting eyes, his pleading smile, his ardent concern to forestall her wishes, and all the idle exhibitions of his preposterous passion. She too
pleased me, but in another way; he was for my
amusement, she for my delectation. It gratified
me to note how she bent him at will: now into
smiles, anon into a decent appearance of solici-

tude, playing upon his admiration as a harper upon chords.   At my table I desired she should so incense my guests, whilst kicking my heels together I might chuckle at my own triumph and their delusion.   (It is odd how one's humour lies so in a balance that another's must fall if it rise.) She had moved from her seat and was passing me with this delirious oaf, when, on a sudden (I presume at a remark of his), she twisted her face into a remarkable grimace.

'Twas not indeed that I hold a grimace beyond the severe limits of beauty; I have known some that were abiding treasures of contempt, astonishment, disdain, or indignation, the most artistical epitomes of these becoming emotions.   But the beauty must needs be assured of her features, and reckon up the chances; such an one and such an one, indeed; but this or that——Pah! to what end is her mirror?   And yet, though I confess the inelegance should have been the measure of my distaste as a man of fashion, as a philosopher I had a deeper surprise and a deeper indignation.   That face awry came upon me as a swift revelation, and through it I pried into all her interior follies.   I had referred unto her certain qualities becoming to so excellent a beauty, and these I now found had been even more instant in my desire of her than her mere bodily attractions.   But this one brief moment had given me a newer, truer insight. Heaven! that I had come so near loving such a

woman! I cannot describe it to you—(my sword
is more at your service than my pen)—but in
that contortion dwelt a score of abject characters.
It was a peephole into her soul, and I thank God
for its opportunity. To have lived with such a
grimace potential had˙been to have dwelt under
an avalanche. I should have looked for it in fear
day by day; its prospect would have been my
terror; in the night beside her apparitions of it
had haunted me like ghosts. Yet this were a
small matter; to the philosopher such an expec-
tation would be as nothing beside the terrible
evidence of her qualities thus manifest. I have
no irreverence in my mind when I say that it had
been purgatory to have housed with a woman of
such flaws. That grimace opened a vista of her
imperfections ; and though I cannot depict them,
they glare upon me each moment I recall it. I
saw her then to be of a humbler construction
than I had thought. Alas! I propound my feelings but weakly ; I shall despair to make you
understand me. A dozen possible vulgarities
lurked round her mouth ; lapses innumerable
gleamed in her eyes; and for the shape of her
face—it was past the semblance of loveliness. In
that grimace her character was exhibited, and my
own fatuity made public.

The philosophy of this fortunate˙disillusion-
ment is most manifest to an astute thinker. It
is a common error to suppose that the object of

the affection glorifies her own actions; that from
the love flows a divine halo to encircle all the
properties of the beloved. It was so perhaps
with the raw passions of our ancestors; it may
even be so with certain backward types of our
own day; but true wisdom is certain of nothing.
To be cajoled, indeed, by a pretty seeming were
easy even for the wisest, but haply there will
come a time when the miserable man shall discover his folly. It is this knowledge should set
us on edge to watch the phases ere it be too late.
I am not of those who hold, as they barbarously
phrase it, that it is chiefly the animal we regard
in woman. Affection upon such a basis were
rightly unreasonable and fatuous. But to them
that seek the soul within the precincts of beauty
love wears another guise. And that soul (who
shall deny?) is portrayed amply in the bodily
phenomena; from which the sage may gather
how earnestly the tricks, gestures, and facial
expressions of the sex must be regarded. In one
look he shall see nothing but the modest habit
of innocence, and if he go no further he will
swear she be virtue incarnate. In another there
will be pride, and a little pride is most commend-
ing to a man of fashion; in yet another, humour
—a gift of excellence upon a dull evening, when
there is no news in the town; again, timidity,
which a man shall find tempting in a woman; or
once again, an affectation sufficiently engaging.

But if these fascinations breathe through her frequent public expressions, can you say (without due care) that she hides not as many defects ? A shrewishness, the love of gossip, a leaning unto spite, an affection for the vulgar, a ribald temper, a distressing appreciation of the table, a pretentiousness, an indelicate desire of laughter : all these and more may be betrayed in looks, in gestures, in motions—in a grimace. I thank Heaven for my warning, and am constrained to feel some kind of pity for the frenzied fellow to whom my timely withdrawal has assigned her, and who now boasts himself (poor fool !) the happiest in my acquaintance.

OVER THE FIRE

TO them that have no fears of the narrow house, winter is a time of keener pleasures than any of the three remaining seasons. I think, indeed, it is pretty amply redeemed by its own idiosyncrasies. Its very vices provoke their own defeat, and call forth conditions which lay them into insignificance. Of its ill purpose there can be no doubt; its slow and shuffling gait, its noxious breath, its little sneaking round of spites, smack all of malignity. You can see its withered arms itching for action from the back of September where it jostles with the melancholy autumn. It is thanks to no mercy of the season, but to your own fortitude alone, that you can clear the corner and come safely into spring. But we are happily armed with some compensation for those treacheries, and so live through the winter pretty securely in our trenches. The evil humours of this Septentrion prey upon the weaker bodies; for the more part, though we keep at odds, we exact therefrom many definite

pleasures and one particular ecstasy. Each
season has its individual habits, proper to the
respective rigours, and by these our human kind
maintains itself in harmony with its circumstances,
and derives from these its separate delights.
But this particular ecstasy of which I speak is a
character of the fourth alone. It will sound odd,
perhaps paradoxical and flush of sentiment; it is
irrational, I know; it is certainly a most immaterial enjoyment; and yet in one mood not
uncommon to a man of cares, there is a finer zest
in dreaming at the fire than may be got from any
employment or recreation from term to term of
the rolling year.

It is this touch of superterrene fancy that
makes winter the most romantical of seasons.
There is something unessential to earth in a fireside reverie, whence or how deriving I know not.
You will have, of course, the gross comfort of
creature warmth in cover from a snowing or
a streaming sky; but this is intelligible and
human, very welcome and soothing against the
outrageous elements. It is in the mind you will
feel the subtilest delight. Your hands rubbing
at your knees, your body relaxing in a gentle
glow, your eyes set with some gratitude upon the
occasion of your comfort, you will drift and pass
into another world: a world of the rarest
illusions, a world of exquisite and intangible
thoughts and fancies. To say you are building

castles in the embers is to interpret your dreams heinously : you will never see in the fire one single vision that ministers to your vulgar ambitions or aspirations. Wealth and prosperity, long life and happiness—these have no place in the suggestions of the fire ; nor, indeed, has any passion common to the streets. The sights and visions are too delicate, too fleeting for utterance, even for distinct comprehension. The flames transfigure all. When you enter therein you leave the world of coherence and form behind you, and live only with impalpable presences and undefined desires. There are castles and palaces, it is true, glimmering through diaphanous veils of mist ; there are caverns beyond caverns of mystical light reaching from space to space till they vanish in the glowing recesses. But these fabrics are unsubstantial and recall no memory of the earth, being of faëry, and released from all mundane laws and conditions. What reason can there be for this strange transition ? In the red heart of the fire alone does sorcery linger ; and here alone it is possible to be made free of exigent time, and to turn Space into Infinity. All that is illimitable and eternal pervades the thoughts that rise with the flames. The mind assumes the quality of a mirror, and reflects each momentary change of the ashes with sensitive precision. In a minute you will have suffered as many sensations as in other times would crowd a life. There is no

stability nor rest in the ethereal construction of
the embers, and your mind, too, wanders on wings.
The stream of fancies sweeps in a luminous pageant over you: the breath comes and goes, and
with each inspiration a hundred formless imaginings have fled. You can behold wonders in the
fire. You may see the universe in ruins, and your
life reverted and resolved; spirits may appear to
you in the flickering tongues; you may be rapt
up to catch a glimpse of Deity itself. And whatever marvels pass before you, these fantasies—so
swift, so instant, as to slip the nimblest mind—
leave by their passage a sweet and thrilling contentment, a self-sufficient ecstasy. You will perceive that you are communing with a higher
sphere, are admitted to a transcendent company.
At times some faint memory seems to mingle with
your sensations, as though they were the issue of
your own past: a recollection descends with a
thrill upon you; flashes and is gone. The gates
of your soul swing open for an instant; but ere
your eye can spy with certainty upon the inner
sanctuary it has clapped to again, and you are
left to wonder on your own secrets. How much
is there in the spirit of man without his knowledge? Is it that in these moments he makes a
vague contact with a superior consciousness, in
fits, in gushes, in irregular spasms? There is, at
least, no wit sufficient to track to its fount this
intermittent flow of royal condescension. As an

arrow in the air, as a swallow through the sky, so thought upon thought takes flight out of the void into the void, leaving vacancy behind. The motes of fancy glitter in the mind, impalpable, luminous, and innumerable. They impress the soul with a certain mark, and sail forthwith out of vision. Your hold upon your own mind is at this time very insecure, and you flutter with the flames in and out of sanity. For to feel and to be unable to refer your feeling to its components is to verge on madness. Now you will have a floating sensibility of something dear and familiar; remembrance comes at a call to your elbow; and then the flash has gone, and the unknown, the unknowable, the ineffable, that which lies beyond sense of touch or sight or audience, gleams, an instantaneous spark, in the shadows of your soul.

And thus the phantasmagoria passes, until the white embers fall and fade and turn suddenly to red; and the red pales behind its feathered coat of ashes, leaving you confronted and encompassed by the monstrous verities of this boreal and laborious life. Gone are your serene and mystical dreams, and there lie the ashes—grey, elemental, most comprehensible, rudely tangible, dust and rubbish for the broom.

O-DAY the Spring is in my heart—
the Spring and its roses. The fumes
of the morning have mounted into
my senses; the blood runs in little
gushes of delight through my body.
Yet with all this intoxication I am sober enough
to think upon the courses of the sun and to see
the world with the eyes of wisdom. This is the
time of roses. It is true enough that the flowers
no longer have their seasons; but each still makes
an ample exhibition at its own particular point
of the year. Our artificers of the garden have
stolen from us the individual enchantment of the
months; these no longer enjoy their divine rights,
but slip by now without distinctive gait, with no
private gaieties of their own, an equable procession of good-natured visitors lacking their proper
spites and ecstasies. It was the flowers that marked
the time of the year; and now from January to
December our clock is broken, and we must set
our lives by the stars. Once my love had lived

222

through twenty summers of the rose, and now
she must take her age from the sun. We may
pick our roses now in the snows of Christmas as
appropriately and as casually as upon May-Day.
This despotic abolition of our calendar would
have been welcome had it kept the sun in the
heaven, and left us unchanged our vicissitudes in
the garden; but we cannot live our time out
under frames, and as yet we lack the secret of
the rains. And to rob these periods of their
emblems is, as it were, to rob a house of its
scutcheon, a woman of her honour; certainly to
rob the year of its history. We have plundered
the returning moons of their birthrights, and it
is now only by the profusion of its offerings that
a season protests against the monstrous violation
of its natural law.

In June, it may be, is the grand climacteric of
the rose; then she blows and swells into her
maturer proportions, her fuller fragrance. But
our summers live hard in these days, and, do we
get that solstice at all, we are by mid-year
steeped in its favours and asweat with its gifts;
and the rose is overblown. May, if she come in
her own apparel, is a fresher, fairer time, as is this
May of mine. Her flowers have bourgeoned, but
they have still the dew of the morning upon
them, they still disperse the odour of the Spring-
time. This truly is the proper dawn of the

year, and wears the face of youth, even in this
old and veteran city. To-day I have put by the
prodigious achievements of human art, and am
living in the supreme hour of the rose. The
town is ablaze with roses; the very streets and
houses breathe them to my nostrils. For I have
risen with the whimsey in my head, and all
Nature is one blushing rose. The air is scented
with the summer rain; the squares are joyous.
There comes my mistress with a red rose at her
bosom this merry morning. Drops sparkle between the petals; she wears the first white garment of the year; everywhere is a rose—a rose.
It laughs in her eyes, which are blue as the
violet; it blooms in her cheeks, which are pink
as a daisy; on my faith, it is in her lily-white
brow, it tosses with her brown hair. Her lips—
when were not lips a rose to a lover? The shops
are a masque of roses, but her rose is the rose for
me. Upon their stems the flowers hang sedately,
reticent within their leaves, modest apparitions
of grace; but, plucked and shining on her breast,
they are endued with a new courage, informed
with a fresh pertinence, and inspired with the
zeal of their comely dwelling-place. She herself
is their exemplar, and to adorn her is to wither
with honour. But as my love trips towards me
there is no thought of death this dewy morning.
Her soul creeps up the sky to the meridian, and

in the light and warmth of her being the roses
bud and blow in her possession. To-day the
morning rings with gaiety. If you would see
Aurora newly lighted upon the earth with her
sweet dimples, here is the vision at your doors,
ye modern men of London! There are no softer
smiles than hers, there is no shyer ecstasy. Each
step makes music in her ears; each glance espies
battalions of delight; with each breath she has
thrills of the world and its mystery. No thought
interrupts the sprightly march of her sensations;
life throbs in her body; and the rose is dancing
over her heart to the beat of her gaieties.

On this rosy morning the flowers are vivid on
their bunches. They wake and stir together, one
might say; they, too, have the spirit of youth.
And this rose on the bosom of my mistress, afire
with its pride of place, grows garrulous and
jocund, and lives at the heat and pace of fever.
See now, as she nears me, how it calls in its
exhilaration to the roses in her face! In and out
they blow and fade, trepidant and precipitate;
here with a quiver, gone with a shake, in fitful
and bewildered answer to the summons from
below. 'Fuller and ever fuller'—the crimson
swells and shrinks, flames and falters. Like a
flaw upon the sea a stain of red starts up and
spreads over her cheek; at her white bosom is
that patch incarnadine—the red, red rose. Agi-
tant and tremulous it has burst open, and its pure

heart lies bare. It has lived its life through this merry May morning, but the dew and the fragrance still linger in its petals, as the happy tears on the eyelids of my beloved now she lies in my arms, with her roses.

THE FACILITY OF LIFE

IT has in all times been a part of our creed to think sadly upon our human estate, which is the gift of God, and to consider ourselves no better than bondmen till we be free of our carnal husk. The growing voice of ages has proclaimed this wretched investiture of flesh to be a continuous evil, so that with the cloud of witnesses we have come to take it for a common axiom of life. Yet upon the facts this would seem a foolish assumption, and may indeed be rebutted as an error of the supersensitive. Perhaps it is the Christian faith that has most favoured the error; yet such as Socrates had the same thought, and we should rather regard it as succeeding naturally to a sympathetic contemplation of human suffering. So long have our philosophers impressed upon us that we live at war, in a plenitude of sorrows and losses, distraught with the horrors of our environment, agape upon the sudden breaches in our immediate ranks, that almost any one of us may now, upon

provocation, fall to tears at the moral of it. And yet were it only true that man had this agony of life for a constant purview, poor Nature had long since succumbed to the wretched neighbourhood; there had been no duty more sacred, as no prospect more inviting, than the release of the frail tenant from the frailer clay. Philosopher and theologian have held life to be nothing but a toilsome pilgrimage to some peaceful bourne—it may be Paradise, or haply oblivion. The balance (they have both declared) is against us here; but (quoth the one) it shall be readjusted upon the dissolution of our mortal frame; while the other has looked oftener to a restitution in the conclusion of death. Must we, then, confess to this grotesque subservience to a shadowy faith, or to a grim patience? Surely, were the balance ever against us, the soul had determined its own miseries upon the first appreciation of the horrid iniquity. We are surely to say that there are all but none to whom this existence has sincerely seemed intolerable; nay, that there are few that have not judged it, at the worst, a pleasing tragicomedy with an impertinent ending. Yet should you go by their open professions this were not so. How glibly falls from the tongue the deprecation of a thing so shameful and unworthy! It is possible to take no pride in life, if we be rightly minded. At each turn we hold up our hands and lengthen our faces upon the knowledge that we are still in travail. We shake our heads upon a calamity, remarking how truly sorrow is our portion. But withal this profession is, as it were, a mere habit of the outward features, as you may grimace at the conception of a pain you have not felt. In the life it is but an hypothesis, a supposition of our fathers which it is seemly to acknowledge upon decent occasions.

Were a proof of this assertion needed you would find it in the very fact of life; for that cannot be odious which all use with such affection. We cannot doubt that, were this vain repetition true, humanity had effaced itself, for it is clear man has never lacked spirit for a desperate act. But perhaps, you will say, it is not from fear of death the race is withheld from this obliteration, but rather by the hope of a fortune that never befalls. This hope, you may urge, and not a real preponderance of happiness, keeps us from the desire of that final equilibrium. And were this so, is not hope also an integral part of the human equipment, to be reckoned in the general sum of our substantial pleasures? Being of our carnal endowment, this too must go into the scales against evil. And in the higher natures, I doubt not, so subtle a property must raise a formidable barrier 'twixt life and death; though, unhappily, it is also so ethereal that upon a change it may dissolve and leave clear a sudden access. But it is not hope inspires the most of us with content; it is rather the immediate and manifest delights of living. And how many there are if we rightly divine them! The whole journey is to the last full of opportunities of happiness for mind and body, though some so fatuously ignore them. It is here, in truth, while we thrust our hideous ancestry from our rarer minds, we yet derive from it our greatest blessing; for it is only so far as we are of common clay with the brute that we can forget and enjoy. The brute proceeds upon his grosser pleasures with a blind complacency from which our finer natures, an ineffectual compromise between God and him, shrink and wince. It is to such as he, nevertheless, we owe our desire of life. For to forget and to enjoy—these are the capacities that serve us best, and these are of the brute's prerogative. To those of human kind that have these fulfilled life can be nothing but an ample satisfaction; to him that has his just share of them life is this tolerable affair I have said. The joys of living may, indeed, be of no great proportions, but they are ever-recurrent, small, unexpected, immediate, grateful. You would account them meagre and unsatisfying did you regard them as a philosopher; yet by their continuous passage they yield a sense of repletion. You will gather a score of them ere you rise; they will pursue you all day if you have eyes for them; they are incessant and multitudinous. The flesh wherewith you are clothed

will exult in them, if you will permit; the mind
will passively absorb them.   They are in your
delicate senses, in your gentle meditations, in your
books, in the air, everywhere.   Is the wind soft,
it is a charm; be it chill, how brightly burns the
fire; does it snow, you may admire a white world!
You must snatch these delights from the hour,
neither remembering evil nor forecasting; you
must train your mind to the habit; your senses
must be alert; you must laugh; you must be
content; you must forget.   There is always
magic in the air if you will forget.

It is this forgetfulness which is, after all, the
foundation of our pleasures, for in memory is the
weightier part of our misfortunes.   Of a truth in
the course of our journey many pains befall, and
there are times of gross evil, when sorrow, as a
toad, squats in our doorway, when the scales kick
the balance with a rush.   In such an hour we
come to look upon life as the dreary passage of
our commonplaces; there is neither present gain
nor future hope.   But how soon this mood
passes! From our base ancestry we have the
divine gift of forgetfulness.   In a little we are
upon our way again, a lessening memory at our
backs; growing ruddy and merry, laughing, de-
riding, scoffing, enjoying, taking the blandish-
ments of the moment with a heart of the lightest.
And thus do we trip along the road, with a lapse
here and there (in a trice forgotten), until we are

come to the verge ; and lo, how short has been the journey which once stretched out so far ! how pleasant the way we have feared at times would prove so dreary ! How they all fade, sorrows and pains and memories ! and upon the verge how finite they seem against the eternal ! Life is very facile to animals ; it is facile also to the supreme animal.

Printed by T. and A. CONSTABLE, Printers to Her Majesty
at the Edinburgh University Press.